3/90

MITCHELL PARK BRANCH

Palo Alto City Library

OUTER
SPACE
AND ALL THAT
JUNK

BY MEL GILDEN

J.B. LIPPINCOTT NEW YORK

Library of Congress Cataloging-in-Publication Data
Gilden, Mel.
    Outer space and all that junk / by Mel Gilden.
        p.   cm.
    Summary: A boy works for his uncle one summer only to discover
him collecting junk in the belief he is helping aliens return to their
home in outer space.
    ISBN 0-397-32306-9 : $ — ISBN 0-397-32307-7 (lib. bdg.) :
$
    [1. Science fiction.   2. Extraterrestrial beings—Fiction.]
I. Title.
PZ7.G386Ou 1989   88-37110
[Fic]—dc19   CIP
                                                        AC

For Uncle Dave Linck:
Krel Technician, Mighty Morlock Hunter,
and
Junkman Extraordinaire

TABLE OF CONTENTS

OUTER SPACE
AND ALL THAT
JUNK

CHAPTER ONE
WEIRD OLD UNCLE HUGO

Myron Duberville had heard strange rumors about his old uncle Hugo. His mother said Hugo was okay, but that was not necessarily a recommendation. Myron had doubts about the okay-ness of Mrs. Duberville herself.

Even though his mother was the biggest stockholder in the Astronetics Corporation, she knew less about electronics than most high school kids. And all his mom knew about flying was that when you weren't in first class, you had to pay extra if you wanted a drink of anything stronger than ginger ale. His mom always flew first class.

She and her current boyfriend, Donald, were probably flying first class even as Myron hauled his three big suitcases in a rented hand truck along the crowded concourse of the Vasichvu Bend International Airport. Myron was fourteen years old, but he looked a little older in his gray slacks and hound's-tooth sport coat. Though no one could see it because of the sport coat, on the pocket of the pale-pink golf shirt he wore was a little pelican.

All the best people had pelicans on their pockets, his mother had said. Even though it was silly, knowing the pelican was there gave him confidence. With a summer full of Uncle Hugo staring him in the face, he needed all the confidence he could get.

Myron was passing yet another shop where people were buying magazines and paperback books and wind-up swimming fish and battery-operated barking dogs—it was amazing what kind of stuff normally rational people would buy when they were in an airport—when suddenly a loud beeping came from one of his suitcases. People turned away from the magazines they were pawing through to look at him. He shook his head and pushed his round, black-framed glasses up his nose while he hauled his hand truck to one side of the concourse. A big woman with her mouth wide open was snoring loudly in one of the nearby chairs. The beeping did not disturb her.

Myron pulled the bottom suitcase out onto the floor of the concourse. When he opened it, the beeping immediately got louder. He felt around under more pastel golf shirts, each with a pelican on its pocket, and at last pulled out a black plastic box that was about the size and shape of a candy bar. On the front, a gray lightning bolt was stamped.

He turned his back on the concourse and extended an antenna from the black box. The box squawked at him, and he adjusted a knob on the side. A tinny voice coming out of the box said, "Oh, damn, I never know how to work these things." Then there was a lot of static.

"Mom," Myron said into the box. More static. Louder this time, Myron said, "Mom."

The same tinny voice in the box said, ". . . sure that this is . . ." Then there was more static.

"Mom," Myron said patiently, and tapped the box with one finger. "Mom, can you hear me?"

"OF COURSE I CAN HEAR YOU!" the voice suddenly blasted from the box. Myron immediately turned the knob on the side of the box, but too late. The large woman had awakened and was looking at him angrily. He looked right back at her. Soon the woman got up and shuffled to a nearby refreshment stand.

"Yes, Mom. What can I do for you?"

"Is that you, Myron?"

"Yes, Mom. I have the only radio that can receive a signal from your transmitter."

"Don't be cross with me, Myron. Your father was clever too. But I never could understand this technical stuff."

"I know, Mom." Myron's mom had been telling him for years that she didn't understand technical stuff. It was obviously true. He was a little tired of hearing about it. "Was there anything in particular?"

5

"I'm your mother, Myron. Give me some slack. Donald and I are just about to take off for Aspen. He assures me that the skiing is wonderful this time of year. I just wanted to check and make sure that you were all right."

"I'm all right."

"Your uncle Hugo should be there soon to pick you up."

"I'm sure he will be."

"Despite whatever you've heard, Hugo is a perfectly wonderful human being."

"I'm sure he is."

"It's time the two of you met. You'll have lots to talk about, I'm sure. I'll be back for the big Astronetics stockholders' meeting in two weeks. While I'm gone, pay attention to your uncle Hugo. You can learn a lot from him."

"I'll try, Mom."

"Oh, and I almost forgot. Your little friend Arthur called just after you left. He wanted to know if you could help him with his Advanced Placement Computer project. I told him that you would be with your uncle Hugo in Vasichvu Bend all summer, working for Astronetics."

"I'll have to write Arthur a letter." Myron wondered if Arthur really needed help with some project or if he just wanted another chance to beat Myron at Captain Conquer. Arthur thought playing video games was educational. Myron agreed, but only if you designed them yourself.

"... what? Oh. Myron, I must go. Donald says the pilot refuses to hold the plane any longer. Good-bye. Be good...." Suddenly the static came back, and there was a loud click.

Myron shook his head while he collapsed the antenna and slid the radio into his sport-coat pocket. He arranged the suitcase on the hand truck again, then pulled it a little way down the concourse to a potted palm he had had his eye on.

Myron stuck the radio in among some green hairy stuff around the small palm tree. It looked as if the radio were nesting and had cozied up next to the tree for warmth or companionship. He walked on feeling as if he had accomplished something.

After marching through the terminal for what seemed to be hours, Myron came to the place where he was supposed to meet Uncle Hugo. Uncle Hugo had chosen the spot and the conditions, and neither of them made Myron feel more comfortable about his summer.

First, he was to buy a silver balloon filled with helium. On the side of the balloon were painted the words VASICHVU BEND IS A SUMMER FESTIVAL. With the balloon tugging at his free hand, Myron went to stand in front of the souvlaki stand.

Apparently, souvlaki was some kind of Greek meat they put inside a pita-bread pocket. Actually, the food smelled pretty good to Myron, but he didn't buy a sandwich. Generally, he refused to eat anything whose name he could not pronounce.

He felt pretty silly standing there in front of the souvlaki stand, holding the balloon. He hoped Uncle Hugo would show up soon. And he hoped that being seen with Uncle Hugo would not be even more embarrassing than standing in front of the souvlaki stand holding a silver balloon in his hand.

Myron stood there for about twenty minutes. The smells from the souvlaki stand kept playing with his nose, and after a while he wondered if he had time to eat something before Uncle Hugo showed up. He decided to chance it.

Moments later, he was standing there with a balloon in one hand and a souvlaki sandwich in the other. The sandwich was kind of hard to eat because slices of tomato or onion kept sliding out of it. He was concentrating on pushing his sandwich back together with his tongue when he heard a horn honking.

Myron looked up. He could not believe his eyes. In front of him was a big old truck that looked as if it had been through the wars. It might have been black once. He could not tell exactly what color it was now because it was dented and scuffed and needed a good washing. In fact, someone had written with a finger in the dirt on one fender DIRT TEST. DO NOT WASH.

The back of the truck had high sides, but it was piled even higher with trash, rubbish, and discards—all kinds of junk. There were no old grapefruit rinds or anything slimy like that. But the bed of the truck was loaded with car parts, bird cages, wastebaskets, bicycles without wheels, tires, sprung mattresses, lamps, toasters, and twists of wire and bent metal that Myron could not identify.

The driver leaned across the cab of the truck and shouted out the open window at Myron over the humming of the surprisingly smooth engine. "Are you Myron Duberville?"

No, thought Myron. No. Let this not be Uncle Hugo. Let this just be some nice crazy man who has made a mistake. Please. "Yes," he said. "I am Myron Duberville."

"Delighted to meet you," said the man in the truck. "I'm your uncle Hugo."

CHAPTER TWO
JUNK IS NOT ALL JUNK

Uncle Hugo (there was no longer any point denying his identity) allowed the passenger door to swing open slowly. It moaned as if it hadn't opened for ages, maybe not since the truck was new. He then ran around the front of the truck, unloaded Myron's suitcases from the hand truck, and stacked them neatly on the seat, all the while telling Myron how delighted he was to see him.

Myron did not talk much, pretending that he was very involved with finishing his sandwich. But he did a lot of thinking while he rolled the hand truck to the hand-truck dispenser and got his quarters back.

What Myron thought about was this: His mother had really done it to him this time. She had left him in the care of this junk man while she ran off to have a good time in Aspen with her boyfriend, Donald. She had run off before, but she had always left him in the care of his cousin Judy. Judy and he got along just fine because they left each other alone. Myron could spend the summer reading or designing computer programs. In fact, he could do anything he wanted as long as he kept his feet off the furniture.

Actually, this business with Uncle Hugo was all Myron's fault—which only made him angrier. If he hadn't said that he would like to spend the summer working at Astronetics rather than lying around at Cousin Judy's house, he wouldn't be in the predicament he was in now.

He wiped the last of the souvlaki sauce from his face and hands and threw away the paper napkin. He walked back to the truck, squeezed himself in next to his suitcases, and slammed the door, making it bang hollowly. Uncle Hugo shifted the truck into gear, and with a shake and a roar it entered the stream of heavy traffic. As they bounced along, Myron could feel big metal springs beneath the thin pebbled plastic of the seat.

Uncle Hugo was a careful driver. He was so careful, in fact, that soon a line of cars was bunched up behind him, honking at him, encouraging him to go faster. Myron slid down in his seat so that no one would see him if they looked into the window. Then he studied Uncle Hugo.

Uncle Hugo was a few years older than Myron's father would have been, had he not gone off to South

America to explore and never come back. His thinning white hair was combed straight back—with his fingers, if Myron's observations of his habits were correct. He wore half glasses—little framed half-moons of glass—that were perched down at the tip of his nose. At the moment, he was wearing big clunky shoes and jeans and a work shirt with the sleeves rolled up to the elbows.

Uncle Hugo had a kind face, Myron decided, but it was a little wild and excited, as if he were a kid visiting a circus midway for the first time and he didn't know where to begin looking.

After Uncle Hugo had maneuvered through the airport traffic and was out on a Vasichvu Bend city street, he continued to drive slowly and keep his eyes peeled. Myron said, "Astronetics not doing too well?"

"Why do you ask that?"

"Well," said Myron, uncertain about how direct he could be, "this is not exactly the vehicle I'd expect the chairman of the board of a successful corporation to drive."

Uncle Hugo laughed good-naturedly. "No, no. We have many large government contracts. Your father would have been proud and your mother has nothing to worry about. Of course, most of the contracts are for secret projects so I can't tell you what they are. But this truck has nothing to do with them. It is part of something else entirely, a pet project of mine." He looked at Myron from the corner of his eye and smiled.

Myron waited to see if Uncle Hugo would explain further. He did not, and at last Myron said, "Pet project?"

Uncle Hugo did not answer. Instead, he cried out, "Over there!" and pointed to the sidewalk. Myron hung on tight as Uncle Hugo dived across three lanes of traffic to the curb. Horns honked and tires squealed behind them.

Uncle Hugo leaped from the truck and one by one began to pick up bits of rubbish that were gathered in a sloppy pile on the curb. He took a close look at a typewriter with its keys mashed in, a TV set with bent rabbit ears, and a twisted eggbeater, completely ignoring the worn-out couch, the broken dish drainer, and the pieces of lamp. All the time he smacked his lips as if he were anticipating with gusto the taste of some exotic dish.

Myron tried to pretend he didn't know Uncle Hugo. He was not entirely successful at this. After all, he was sitting right there in the junk truck. Still, he did his best. He looked the other way.

Because he was looking the other way, he saw a strange thing. He saw a woman so busy staring at Uncle Hugo, she didn't watch where she was going, and she drove her old white car right into a light pole across the street. She'd been going pretty slow, so not much damage was done. Still, the collision had made a loud crash. Uncle Hugo never even looked up.

Myron was not surprised to see the woman leap from her car. She was about Uncle Hugo's age, and was the color of coffee with cream.

She walked to the front of her car, her flowered dress flapping in the breeze, but instead of mournfully studying her punched-in front end and shaking her head as any normal person might have done, she went down on her knees and began to stroke the light pole as if it were a sick child.

The woman was obviously some kind of a wacko. At first Myron wondered what sort of institution she had escaped from. Then he thought he ought to go see if she needed any help. But soon a crowd gathered and he knew someone else would help her. Myron was relieved. He was involved with one wacko already, and that was enough.

The woman stopped stroking the light pole and stared across the street at Uncle Hugo again. She was about to cross the street herself when the police arrived and began to ask her questions.

Uncle Hugo got into the truck carrying the twisted eggbeater in his hand. With apparent satisfaction he said, "I got one." Still clutching the eggbeater, he started the truck and drove off without a second look at the black woman and her accident.

"You see, Myron, the work never stops." Uncle Hugo sighed. "You can be a big help to me this summer."

"A big help? Mom said I'd be working at Astronetics."

Uncle Hugo waved away Myron's words as if they were so many flies. "Yes, yes, of course. That's all settled. I meant that you could help me with my pet project." Uncle Hugo pursed his lips and nodded.

"What exactly is your pet project, Uncle Hugo?"

Uncle Hugo peered at him instead of the road long enough for Myron to wonder how long it would be before they too ran into a light pole. At last Uncle Hugo looked out the windshield and said, "It's kind of a goodwill situation, actually." He nodded to himself again and added, "I'm finding aliens and sending them home."

"Aliens?" said Myron. "You mean like refugees from El Salvador? Like that?"

"No," said Uncle Hugo. "I mean aliens from other planets."

Wacko, thought Myron. I'm trapped in this truck with a wacko. He wondered how long it would take him to hitchhike to Aspen.

Uncle Hugo's house was normal enough for a mansion, Myron thought. It was huge and stood at the end of a long sweeping driveway. Acres of grass and trees surrounded the place. The smell of freshly cut grass filled the air. Myron immediately felt he could do a lot of exploring here. Despite his feelings about Uncle Hugo, Myron liked where he lived.

Uncle Hugo parked his junk truck right in front of the mansion. He ran up the wide front steps while he called, "Osgood! Osgood, where are you?"

At the front door, Uncle Hugo met a small bald-headed man who had a worried look on his face. He was dressed very formally in a suit with tails and gold buttons. "Oh, Osgood," Uncle Hugo said to the small man, "please help Myron get his bags up to the guest room. Make him comfortable in any way you can. I'll be in the library." He shook the eggbeater in Osgood's face and went into the house.

Myron was pulling his suitcases out of the truck while Osgood marched down the stairs. Osgood got one suitcase under an arm and carried each of the other two by its handle. Myron followed him up the stairs.

Beyond the big white door was a long hallway wide enough to play basketball in. Closed doors lined the hallway, and at the far end, a big stained-glass window of a robot let in sunlight. On the walls were paintings of people in strange costumes. A few looked familiar. "Fifty years of movie and television aliens," Osgood explained. Myron could not tell from Osgood's tone of voice how he felt about the paintings.

Nor could he tell how Osgood felt about the things Myron saw hanging from the ceiling on wires as he climbed the big main staircase. Each was a spaceship of some kind. Imaginary spaceships like the Starship Enterprise were right there, bow to jet, with real spaceships like the space shuttle. There seemed to be hundreds of different models.

As Osgood led Myron along the second-floor hall-way, he still had that worried look on his pudgy face. Myron wondered if he ever lost it. He wondered if, after living with Uncle Hugo for a while, he might not have a perpetually worried look on *his* face too.

Osgood led Myron to a closed door. It opened like a regular door, but behind it was another one, made of some kind of white plastic stuff. Osgood set his palm on a blue handprint next to the door, and it slid aside.

Beyond the two doors was one of the strangest rooms Myron had ever seen in his life. Osgood set down the suitcases while Myron looked around.

The large room was paneled in the same white plastic stuff as the door. Between the thick plastic sheets were red stripes. There were no lamps or light fixtures in the room, but the walls glowed with a soft, pleasant luminescence. Instead of windows, there were spaces that looked like blank TV screens. The furniture was rounded and looked as if it were made of the same stuff as the walls. A few chairs were scattered around the room but Myron saw no bed. On one wall was a big digital clock that read out the time, the phase of the moon, the air temperature (Fahrenheit and Celsius), and the barometric pressure.

"This is my room?" asked Myron. He picked up a book from a small table. It was by someone named

Willy Ley and was called *Exotic Zoology*. Myron sighed.

Osgood said, "It is indeed, Master Duberville. It is an exact copy of the captain's cabin in the fantastically popular science-fiction film *Skyjacks of the Universe*, written and directed by Harve Fishbein. Your uncle Hugo thought you would enjoy sleeping here."

"But there's no bed."

For answer, Osgood passed his hand over the same small table that held the books. Instantly, a slit opened in the wall next to the table, and a wide shelf thrust out from it. The shelf was made up as a bed. "I remember now," said Myron. "Just like in the movie."

"Your uncle Hugo is nothing if not a stickler for accuracy."

Osgood lifted a suitcase to the bed and began unpacking it. "I hope you will be comfortable here," he said.

Myron shook his head and said, "I'm not sure yet that I'm staying."

Osgood gave him a worried look but continued to lay out Myron's clothing and hang it up. Myron continued to be unsure, but he did not stop Osgood. The closet was behind another sliding door. "Does this place come with a book of instructions?" he asked.

"Your uncle Hugo thought you might enjoy puzzling the room out for yourself."

"That sounds like Uncle Hugo. What exactly is wrong with him?"

18

"Wrong, sir?"

"You know, Osgood. This business about aliens, and all these spaceships and fancy rooms." He shook *Exotic Zoology* at Osgood. "These books."

Osgood shook his head. He glanced from side to side, then leaned toward Myron and whispered, "To tell you the truth, sir, he's never been the same since the moon landing."

Why was Osgood whispering? Was it working for Uncle Hugo that had made him so weird and secretive? Myron sat down gingerly on the bed, hoping that it would not roll back into the wall by itself. He gripped the book in his hands but did not look at it.

Osgood walked to the door, turned, and said, "Is there anything else?"

"Not at the moment."

"Dinner is at six, sir."

Myron didn't say anything as Osgood let himself out through the two doors. He looked at the other books on the table. There was a book about alien encounters, a book about UFO landings, and a copy of Robert Heinlein's *Have Space Suit—Will Travel*. Myron had actually read that one. He opened it up and began to flip the pages. He closed it again when he saw that every instance of the phrase "Mother Thing" had been underlined.

Gloomily, he wondered whether Uncle Hugo's craziness ran in the family. Maybe it was some kind of curse, and Myron would soon be a wacko too. Maybe wanting to work for Astronetics was the first symptom!

Myron wanted answers, and he wasn't getting them sitting on this trick bed. He threw the Heinlein novel back on the stack and went downstairs.

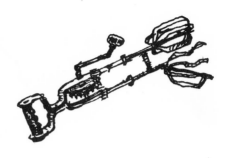

CHAPTER THREE
IT'S STRICTLY A SOUND
BUSINESS PROPOSITION

Myron stood at the foot of the stairs thinking. He didn't know what he was looking for. Something to prove that he wasn't crazy? Something to prove that Uncle Hugo wasn't crazy? Right now, Myron would settle for either.

The house was very quiet. He heard nothing but the ticking of a clock and some dry clicking noises that seemed to be coming from behind one of the doors off the main hallway. He was about to knock on the door when he heard someone clear his throat.

Myron followed the sound and came to the kitchen, a huge tiled room that had pots and pans hanging from racks along the walls. All the tile was yellow. The stove was black and enormous, big enough to roller-skate on. A chopping block made from a tree stump took up most of the center of the room. Off to one side, Osgood sat at an enamel-topped table drinking what smelled like coffee.

Osgood looked up at him worriedly, but that didn't bother Myron. He now knew that Osgood always looked worried. "Settling in nicely, Master Duberville?" Osgood asked.

"Settling in? Oh sure. Say, do you think Uncle Hugo would mind if I explored the grounds?"

"I'm sure he wouldn't. But remember that dinner is at six."

"I won't forget," Myron said, already halfway out the back door.

The backyard was so big, it looked like a public park. At one end of the big grassy plot were some tennis courts. The nets hung in shreds. Evidently, Uncle Hugo had no interest in tennis. At the other end was a brick barbecue. Myron ignored the barbecue and the tennis courts and walked straight across the grass toward a small forest of trees.

It was pleasant under the trees, dim and smelling of green things. Wind occasionally rustled the leaves, and when it didn't, Myron could hear birds and insects that he couldn't even see as they went about their business.

Quite a change from what Myron was used to in the city where he lived with his mom. He realized this was probably the first time in his life that he could not hear traffic. An airplane humming far overhead was the only mechanical sound he heard, and that was so far away, it sounded like an insect.

Myron crunched through dead leaves and came at last to a gravel road. It could not be a public road; this was still Uncle Hugo's property, Myron was sure. He looked along it both ways but saw only more grass, more trees, more hedges. It was all very pleasant but not very helpful.

He spit into the palm of his hand, then struck the spit with a finger of his other hand. The spit pointed to the left. That was the way he walked.

He walked for a while, the gravel making a friendly noise beneath his shoes. It was very loud in the rustic silence. Soon he came to a mountain of junk piled at the side of the road. It was as big as a small house, and looked as if it had been thrown together from the same kind of broken mechanical stuff Uncle Hugo carried around in the back of his truck. Myron picked up a hanger and flung it higher up the mountain, where it stuck in a rusty bedspring. Evidently, Uncle Hugo had been collecting junk for a long time.

Myron shook his head. Wacko, he thought glumly. Somebody ought to make a movie about us: *Curse of the Wackos* or *The Fall of the House of Duberville*. Everybody likes a good horror movie.

When he rounded the junk mountain, he saw a small building in the distance at the end of the gravel road. He walked faster, curious. In real horror movies, the outbuildings of an estate always contained something awful.

It was a barn. It once had been red, but now the

badly weathered paint was flaked into scraggly feathers. The gravel road led right to it.

Myron walked around it. The windows were boarded up and a really impressive padlock held the double doors closed. He considered pulling a board off a window, but he was afraid that he might get splinters in his hands. Also, he didn't want to tear or soil his clothes. He had to be content with shaking the doors to see if the padlock would fall off. It did not.

There was a big grassy field behind the barn, not nearly as well kept as the park near the house. The grass came up almost to his waist, and when he walked through it, stickers hooked into his pants and socks.

Myron walked for another hour or so, but did not find anything as interesting as the barn or as depressing as the junk mountain. He crunched back along the gravel road, found the place where he had walked among the trees, and returned to the house.

He was determined to ask Uncle Hugo what was in the barn. It had to be something important. Even a wacko wouldn't lock up an empty barn.

When Myron returned to the back door, he carefully wiped his feet on the mat and entered. Osgood was preparing dinner. Myron walked through the kitchen, which now smelled of baked chicken, and into the main hallway.

He approached the door behind which he had previously heard the clicking sounds, and was about to knock when he heard shouting coming from inside. Myron waited a moment, shrugged, then knocked anyway. Someone asked him to come in. He cautiously opened the door and found himself looking into the library.

If anything, the library was worse than the rest of the house—though not quite as bad as the guest room. The basic library was paneled in fine old wood and had a spiral staircase at one end that led to a narrow platform from which one could reach a second level of books.

Myron could see the general outlines of tables, couches, chairs, and desks under the piles of books, but every horizontal space was covered with more junk straight out of a junkyard. A drift of ancient eggbeaters leaned against one wall. Ashtrays were full of old vacuum tubes. Schematics of bedsprings and bicycle wheels leaned against stands that looked very much like tall, thin aliens themselves. Broken-down radios and televisions and movie projectors stood in rows across the back of the room. Pie pans and hubcaps dangled from the ceiling, UFO-like, on the ends of wires.

When Myron entered the room, the two men who had been haranguing Uncle Hugo stopped talking. All three men looked at Myron—Uncle Hugo with pleasure, the other two the way adults look at you when you have interrupted something important.

25

Each of the strangers wore a gray suit and had smooth, perfectly combed hair. One wore glasses and a thin mustache. The other didn't. Other than that, they might have been twins. They had been interrupted while shaking papers in Uncle Hugo's face.

"Oh, Myron," said Uncle Hugo. "Come in. Come in."

Myron took a few cautious steps forward and said, "Uncle Hugo, I have a question about—"

"Not now," said Uncle Hugo. Then he spoke proudly to the two men dressed in gray suits. "Gentlemen," he said, "this is my nephew, Myron Duberville. He will be working at Astronetics this summer. Let's ask him what *he* thinks of my business proposition."

"Really, Hugo," said the man with the glasses and the mustache.

"No, this is a good idea." Uncle Hugo said the word "good" as if it were a brand name. "Myron has his father's common sense. Look at that hound's-tooth sport coat if you don't believe me."

"His golf shirt *does* have a pelican on it," said the man without the glasses and the mustache.

The first man shook the papers in the air and turned his eyes toward the ceiling, searching for strength. "Oh, very well," he said. "Ask him whatever you like. Nothing he says will have the slightest bearing on the case."

Grinning confidently, Uncle Hugo tossed Myron a small bar of white metal. Myron caught it easily. It didn't weigh much. "What do you think of that?" Uncle Hugo asked.

"What is it?"

"It's titanium. Very useful in building airplanes and space vehicles and such. It is very light and very strong. There is a lot of it on Earth, but it is difficult to process. That's what makes it so expensive."

This was the most rational thing Myron had heard Uncle Hugo say. Myron said, "Hm."

"You might very well say 'hm,'" said Uncle Hugo. "Remember I told you that I was finding aliens and sending them home?"

Myron nodded. Evidently, for Uncle Hugo, rationality was just a passing fancy.

"Well, after the aliens get home, they will send me an entire fleet of spaceships. And what do you think the cargo aboard those ships will be?"

"Titanium?" asked Myron.

"That's right, my boy," said Uncle Hugo softly as Myron handed the metal bar back to him, "titanium." He leaned back in his chair and said, "You see, it's strictly a sound business proposition. What do you think of it?"

"Before the boy says anything," said the man with the glasses and the mustache, "he should know that these documents"—he shook the papers in Myron's face—"represent thousands of dollars in bills charged to Astronetics. Bills for absolute *junk!* Bedsprings! Spavined bicycles! Dead toasters! Absolute junk! If your

27

uncle Hugo doesn't give up on this business proposition of his, we—Mr. Pinch and I—will, on behalf of the stockholders, have him declared incompetent to run Astronetics."

Myron looked at the others. They looked at him, waiting for an answer. He glanced down and saw a book on top of a stack. The word CLASSIFIED was stamped on the front in gold. Below that it said, *Project Bluebook.* Myron had heard of *Project Bluebook.* It was a government report on flying saucers. He looked at the pie pans and hubcaps dangling from the ceiling.

"I'm just a kid," Myron said. "I don't know anything about this stuff."

The two men in the gray suits nodded as if this answer were just what they had expected from him. Uncle Hugo bowed his head as if he were either praying or ashamed. He looked up and said firmly, "You two get out. We'll discuss this another time."

"You can be sure of it," the first man said. He gathered up his papers and stalked out.

Mr. Pinch said, "At the stockholders' meeting," and followed the other man. Myron could hear Osgood getting them their coats and wishing them each a nice day.

"Maybe that was a mistake after all," Uncle Hugo said.

"*Are* you spending Astronetics money on junk?" Myron asked Uncle Hugo sternly.

"Don't use that tone to me," snapped Uncle Hugo. Myron chewed on the inside of his lip. Though the question he'd asked was a good one, he knew you couldn't talk harshly to a grown-up—especially one who was a wacko—without terrible things happening afterward. He was relieved when Uncle Hugo went on in a friendlier voice, "I don't suppose that was the question you had for me when you came in."

"No, sir. I wanted to know about that old barn at the end of the gravel road."

Uncle Hugo surprised Myron by smiling, and charged around his desk at him. He grabbed Myron by the shoulder and ushered him out of the room. "Come on then, Myron. Maybe you should see it before those lawyers and marketing experts get ahold of you tomorrow."

"Dinner is at six," Osgood cried to them as Uncle Hugo hustled Myron briskly out the back door.

Uncle Hugo knew a more direct route to the barn. He led Myron along a red-brick path on the far side of the tennis courts. It eventually led to the gravel road but much closer to the barn than Myron had expected.

Uncle Hugo refused to answer any more of Myron's questions. He said, "I will explain everything when you see what is in the barn."

He unlocked the big padlock and with Myron's help pulled open the doors. Something big and shiny hulked in the dark interior of the barn. Uncle Hugo walked inside and beckoned Myron to follow.

A stale smell, compounded of animals that had not been there for years and of hay that had, made Myron sneeze. His nose continued to tickle, but he tried to control himself.

Uncle Hugo reached up and pulled a chain that turned on a long row of fluorescent lights in the ceiling. Zillions of dust motes floated in the light. Hay was strewn all over the barn. Some of the walls between the stalls were broken or leaning to one side.

In the middle of the barn was an automobile. It was white and shiny and reflected the bright ceiling light. The chrome looked new. From the size and placement of its fins, Myron knew that the car was many years old. But someone, probably Uncle Hugo, had been taking care of it. Oddly enough, Myron had seen a car like this lately. It looked like the one the crazy woman had run into the light pole.

Uncle Hugo allowed Myron to walk around the car for a few moments before he said anything. The interior was neat and clean, but simple. In the backseat was a pile of junk. Myron recognized a fire hydrant, the tops of several models of streetlights, gum-ball machines, a toaster or two, and boxes of electronic parts. On top of the pile was the eggbeater that Uncle Hugo had picked up earlier that day—or one just like it.

Myron was beyond being surprised by the presence of the junk. He realized now it was just more fuel for the fire over which Pinch and the other man would sacrifice his uncle.

Myron straightened up. Uncle Hugo said, "This is a nineteen sixty Chevrolet Belvedere. It has been specially modified by one of the aliens to fly the entire bunch of them home."

"Which one?" said Myron.

"Which one what?"

"Which one did the modifying?"

"I don't know. One of them there in the backseat. Is it important?"

Myron shrugged. "Probably not. If the ship is ready to go, why is it still here?"

Uncle Hugo said, "You might well ask. I have assembled a fine crew there in the backseat. The only thing I am lacking is a captain. But he'll turn up eventually. Aliens always do. They are like stray animals. The problem is that determining whether you have an alien or just a piece of junk is not always easy until you get it home and see how it acts with the known aliens." Uncle Hugo bent and pointed into the backseat. "See that eggbeater in there? It turned out to be an alien after all. I think it is the gunnery officer."

"Hm," said Myron. Trying not to allow disbelief into his voice, Myron said, "How did you find out all this about the aliens?"

Uncle Hugo ran his hands over the smooth paint job and scratched at a piece of grit with a fingernail. He circled the car, looking at it as if it were a work of art in a museum. He said, "It came to me one day while I was waiting for a cab in front of Astronetics."

"Came to you?"

"Yes. For the first time I noticed the fireplug that had been in front of the building for many years. I took a really good look at it. It was obviously a thing not of this Earth, probably part of a group of aliens who had come to Earth on a trade mission."

"I never heard of any alien trade mission," said Myron with a straight face.

"Exactly," said Uncle Hugo. "That was their problem. Nobody would pay any attention to them. No one even *noticed* them. Is it any wonder that they want to go home?"

Absolutely wacko. If I'm lucky, Myron thought, I will die young and not have to go through the indignity of growing up to be as crazy as my uncle Hugo. Myron said, "So these aliens are all over the place. You are collecting them, ready to send them home."

"That's right. All I'm waiting for is the captain."

"What does the captain look like?"

"You'll know him when you see him," Uncle Hugo said with confidence.

"And you want me to help you collect junk," said Myron.

"I was certain that when you had the whole story, you would be eager to help."

Myron sighed and said, "I don't want to hurt your feelings or anything, Uncle Hugo, but I'd rather work at Astronetics."

Uncle Hugo looked at him gloomily. He said, "Very well." He reached up and pulled the chain again, switching off the light.

Myron helped his uncle close and lock the barn doors. They walked back to the mansion with silence, like a third party, walking between them.

CHAPTER FOUR
A PRINCESS OF ASTRONETICS

The next morning, Myron and Uncle Hugo sat down to breakfast at one end of a long table in the mansion's formal dining room. The table was covered with a red-and-white-checkered tablecloth. Myron ate oatmeal while Uncle Hugo built himself a peanut-butter-and-brown-sugar sandwich. He made a lot of crumbs. Occasionally, he took a knife full of peanut butter from the jar, scraped it onto the side of his finger, and ate it plain. Myron tried not to watch.

A chandelier that hung over the center of the table looked a little strange to Myron. As he ate his oatmeal, he studied it. Soon he noticed that hidden among the glass bobbles and bangles was a model of the Pan Am shuttle craft from the movie *2001*.

Myron had dressed for Astronetics. He was wearing a gray suit similar to the ones that Pinch and the other man had been wearing. His shirt was so white and clean, it seemed to glow. There was no pelican on the pocket of the shirt, but a whole lot of tiny white pelicans in rows decorated his burgundy tie.

Uncle Hugo was dressed much as he had been the day before. He lifted and shook a little bell that had been sitting on the table. Osgood entered the room, patting his mouth with a linen napkin. Uncle Hugo asked for a glass of milk. When Osgood had gone, Uncle Hugo said, "Since you probably don't intend to go hunting for aliens dressed like that, I assume you have not changed your mind."

The night before, while he had lain awake in bed, Myron had thought about what he was going to say to Uncle Hugo in the morning. He'd decided that he would say, "Well, uh, you see, Uncle Hugo, I told my mom that working at Astronetics would be educational. I kinda promised that's what I'd do." And that's what he said now.

Uncle Hugo nodded and said, "It's important to keep your promise. But if you change your mind, please feel free to tell me. I'm sure we can work something out."

They finished breakfast at the same time and walked to the front door together. Uncle Hugo's junk truck was waiting at the bottom of the steps. "Give you a lift?" asked Uncle Hugo.

"No thanks," said Myron. "I think I'll take the bus."

"Suit yourself," said Uncle Hugo.

Myron walked down the driveway swinging his brief-case. He felt confident carrying it, like a real business-man. When he had temporarily been a Cub Scout, he'd imprinted it in gold with his initials and a pelican. Very snappy. As the truck roared past him, Uncle Hugo waved.

The mansions in the neighborhood where Uncle Hugo lived were far apart, and pretty much everybody had a car, so Myron had a long walk to the nearest bus stop. It was across the street from a small white building that was a store called Food and Such. The bus did not come for a long time.

While he waited, watching people go in and out of Food and Such, he reminded himself that he had to write to his friend Arthur. He decided that he would leave out all the parts about Uncle Hugo's strange hobby.

Myron had never actually ridden on a bus before. Usually his mom or Donald took him wherever he wanted to go. Once during a rainstorm he'd even taken a cab. Riding on a bus was kind of an adventure. He bumped along with his briefcase on his knees.

Gee, this is colorful, he thought while he looked around at the people he was riding with. He'd never paid much attention to people who rode buses in real life, but the passengers on this bus could have come right out of movies he'd seen.

Some of them looked very respectable, as if they

were going to some nice job. Others looked as if they hadn't had baths for a long time, as if maybe they lived on the bus. One of those was sitting right behind Myron. Myron could smell him. Another man, anytime he thought no one was looking, snuck a drink from a bottle he kept hidden under a coat that seemed to be more patches than anything else. With a sigh, Myron thought Uncle Hugo would have fit right in.

The new Astronetics building was in an industrial park way across the city from Uncle Hugo's house. Myron had asked the bus driver to tell him when they arrived. What with the traffic and letting people on or off every few blocks, getting to the other side of the city seemed to take hours. By the time the driver called out "Greenbean Avenue," which was where Astronetics was located, Myron had almost forgotten where he was going.

Astronetics was a long two-story building. The industrial park was so new that sprigs of grass were all that grew where the lawn would someday be. Inside, the building still smelled of paint. People rushed everywhere. They were all very intent on what they were doing, which mostly seemed to consist of carrying folders full of paper from one place to another. This was much more like the successful company he had envisioned. He could hardly believe that its chairman of the board was, even as Myron stood there, out collecting junk.

The elevator was blocked off because a man was

fixing it. Myron went over to watch. The man had lowered the elevator car till the top of it was nearly level with the floor. He had taken the cover plate off a piece of machinery on top of the car and was unscrewing something inside. He pulled out the something and looked at it. It was a small metal box on which a little sprocket wheel was caught on a spring-loaded arm. The man pushed a release and let it work once or twice. *Ca-chunk-a. Ca-chunk-a.* The man threw it out of the shaft and almost hit Myron in the foot.

Without thinking Myron picked it up and said, "Do you need this?"

The repairman didn't look up. "Naw," he said. "One of the teeth is missing. If you want it, you can have it."

"Thanks," said Myron, and walked away. He had no idea why he had asked for this whatever-it-was, until it occurred to him that his uncle might like it. Well, Myron *was* staying in his house for free. There was no harm in doing Uncle Hugo a favor, no matter how silly it might seem to Myron. Besides, Uncle Hugo might think that this was the captain. Then he would send his nineteen sixty Chevrolet Belvedere into space and the whole project would be at an end. That would please everybody.

As Myron walked slowly to the main reception desk, he put the whatever-it-was into his briefcase. At the desk he asked for Mr. Lombardi, the head of the Astronetics engineering department.

Minutes later, a girl about Myron's age walked down the stairs as if she were in no particular hurry. His mother would have said she was big-boned or healthy. He knew better. As Arthur would have said, she was a real porker.

She wore jeans and a light plaid shirt. Her short black hair was cut in bangs all the way around and almost touched the tops of the frames of her glasses. She had applied pink lipstick to her lips; it didn't help. She looked familiar, but Myron could not imagine why.

She asked if he was Myron Duberville and he said he was. "You're late," she said.

"I never took the bus before."

"A real working-class hero. Come with me." She led him up the stairs. She looked at him with curiosity as they climbed. When they reached the first landing, she said, "So you're the junk man's nephew."

Myron rolled his eyes. Everybody must know about Uncle Hugo. He would get no peace. He said, "I'm Hugo Duberville's nephew, if that's what you mean."

"We both know what I mean. My name is Princess."

Myron almost laughed out loud, but he gulped the laughter back just in time. Instead, he said, "Hm. Interesting name."

Princess looked at him sharply, then shrugged and said, "Yeah. Myron's an interesting name too."

Myron wondered what she meant by that remark. He was going to get angry but decided it wasn't worth

39

the trouble. A few steps later, he said, "Yeah. I never liked it. Dorky name." Myron walked a little farther away from her. He didn't want her to think that he was agreeing with her because he liked her.

At the top of the stairs, Myron and Princess were at the end of a long hallway that seemed to run the length of the building. They passed big rooms on either side of the hallway, each one filled with long ranks of drafting tables. Each drafting table had a man or a woman humped over it, drawing for all they were worth. Fluorescent lights ran down the hall and out into each room. There were no shadows anywhere. The work area was all very bright and efficient.

Princess said, "My uncle says that a person's name doesn't matter so much as what he does with his life. Of course that's easy for him to say. His name is James."

"I don't think there's a James in my family anywhere," said Myron.

After what seemed to be miles, they turned a corner at the end of the building and came to what Princess called "Officer Country." There were no big rooms here, just tiny offices. The lighting was softer too. Paintings hung on the walls and there was even carpeting on the floors. The paintings did not look like anything in particular, just blotches of color. Most of the office doors were open, each onej revealing a small cubical where a harassed-looking man or woman was making notes on huge sheets of blueprints or speaking excitedly on the phone. Sometimes they were doing both at once.

At a door like all the others, Princess knocked. Next to the door was a painting that looked like a diseased tomato. Someone inside said, "Come in," and Princess led Myron into the room.

This office was much larger than the others he had seen. The man just rising behind his desk was short and dark. His mustache was so small it seemed hardly worth having. Many large photographs covered the walls, each one showing a different airplane and a crew of workers. The man behind the desk was at the center of each picture, dressed each time as he was now, in the gray suit that seemed to be the uniform of executives at Astronetics.

"How do you do, Myron? I'm Mr. Lombardi. We're awfully glad to have you here at Astronetics. I've heard a lot about you from your uncle Hugo." Mr. Lombardi shook hands with Myron and beamed, as if meeting Myron were something he had always longed to do. It was unlikely that his uncle had ever discussed him with Mr. Lombardi, Myron thought, but he did not say so.

"You'll be a messenger just like Princess. Follow her lead and you cannot go wrong."

Moments later, Myron and Princess were back in the hallway. Mr. Lombardi had said little more of value. "If you have a problem, remember, my door is always open," he said as he closed the door.

"He's an engineer?" said Myron with surprise.

"One of the best." As they walked down the hall, Princess went on, "Being a terrific engineer doesn't keep him from being a dork. And vice versa."

Myron spent the rest of the morning following Princess around. She showed him who was working on what project, where the supplies were, how to make a blueprint.

After a few hours, Princess let him off the leash a little. While she went to photocopy a tall stack of calculations, Myron was to carry a roll of blueprints from section 12752 to Mr. Lombardi's office.

Myron found section 12752 just fine, but when he started for Mr. Lombardi's office with the blueprints, he made a wrong turn and immediately was lost. He was sure he had never been in this part of the building before. For one thing, the hallway was painted a bright red. For another, it was deserted except for someone sitting at a desk at the far end of it. Myron would ask him where Mr. Lombardi's office was.

The man behind the desk was wearing a uniform and a silver-plated World War II helmet. When Myron asked him where Mr. Lombardi's office was, the man was not exactly unfriendly, but he was certainly gruff. He didn't know where Mr. Lombardi's office was, but Myron could not come through here. This area was Top Secret, Confidential, and Classified. Myron got the feeling that just by standing there breathing he was breaking any number of government regulations.

Beyond the guard, Myron could see a heavy door. As anyone would, he wondered what was behind it and asked the guard. The guard seemed astonished that Myron had asked, and told him to leave immediately or he would call someone to escort Myron away.

Myron walked back to the other end of the red hall, found where he had gone wrong, and without much trouble found the diseased tomato. He knocked on Mr. Lombardi's door.

Later, Myron caught up with Princess in the room where they hung out when they weren't off on what Princess called a "run." Covering the walls were posters of airplanes for which Astronetics had built systems. Furniture consisted of a couple of plain chairs and a table. Myron asked her what was at the end of the red hallway.

Princess laughed and said, "Funny you should ask. I usually eat lunch there. Did you bring a brown bag?"

Myron admitted that he hadn't.

"No problem. We'll get you a take-out burger from the cafeteria. Then I'll show you the Tea Cup."

About twenty minutes later, Myron was carrying a brown paper bag that had grease stains spreading on it. He followed Princess down corridor after corridor, into strange alcoves and down stairways. They were traveling, Princess said, "into the very bowels of As-tronetics." He was certain that she was right. They descended in a big padded freight elevator, down to where unseen machinery thrummed. The place smelled like chemicals that Myron could not identify. "I hope you know the way back," Myron said.

Princess smiled at him and continued down a dusty narrow stairway. Pipes and conduits ran along the walls and over their heads, sometimes emitting strange clanking noises. They turned corners and went down more stairs. The air became very hot, and later very cold. At the end of a long passageway that was lit by a bare bulb, they came to a door. Next to it was a blue handprint.

"That looks like the lock on my room at home," said Myron with surprise.

Princess said, "Your uncle invented the printlock. I guess he can use one at home if he wants." Princess pressed her palm against the printlock. "Nobody knows where a messenger may have to go on his or her appointed rounds. My handprint can get me in just about anywhere."

"I dunno," Myron said. "This is a secret government place."

"Absolutely. And we're probably not supposed to be here. But whoever set up the security either forgot about this door or didn't know about it. Happens all the time."

She pulled the door open. "But—" Myron began.

"You're not an Agent of a Foreign Power, are you?" said Princess.

44

"Of course not."

"Neither am I." She strode into the corridor beyond. Myron hurriedly followed before the door swung shut.

The corridor led to a dark room. Myron did not know how big it was, but the glowing handprint on the far wall seemed very far away indeed. He ran into Princess.

"Watch where you're going," she said.

"Sorry."

"We have to climb here."

Myron followed Princess up a cold metal ladder. He heard her moving something above, then suddenly a circle of light opened. Myron followed Princess up through it.

CHAPTER FIVE
SOUND ENGINEERING LINES

They were in a white room big enough to hold a jet airplane. When Myron or Princess moved, their foot-steps echoed against the distant walls. The air-conditioning made the room cold enough to raise goose bumps.

In the center of the room was a thing unlike any jet airplane Myron had ever seen. It looked more like a flying saucer. Portholes circled the turretlike body, and a big antenna thrust from the domed top.

"This is the Tea Cup," Princess said. "It is the most secret project at Astronetics."

"Wow," said Myron. "I bet Uncle Hugo loves this thing."

"Absolutely right. That's why he got the Astronetics contract. You should have heard those old fogies on the board scream." Princess approached the awesome vehicle. "I'm hungry. Come on."

Myron followed her to the far side of the Tea Cup, where they climbed a ramp that led into it. The first level of the Tea Cup was divided into rooms the shape of pie slices.

They climbed a ladder in the central open space to the second level. This was one big room; it was obviously the control center of the craft. Chairs stood in front of control boards, each of which had an array of view screens above it. The designer of the control center had obviously watched a lot of *Star Trek* when he was a kid.

Princess sat down in one of the chairs and flicked a few switches. Instantly one of the view screens before her came alive showing a reinforced red door that looked like a spaceship airlock. "That," she said, waving her sandwich at the screen, "is the door that the guard wouldn't let you through. As far as most people know, it's the only way in."

"What if the guard comes in?"

"He won't. He's not allowed to. And nobody else is scheduled to come in here till three this afternoon."

"Neither are we," said Myron, "and we're here."

"We," said Princess, fixing Myron with a bright eye, "are special."

Myron settled down in a chair next to her and together they ate their lunches. After eating a few bites of his burger, Myron said, "Where'd you get a name like Princess?"

She looked at him, checking to see if he was being

nasty, or if he really wanted to know. "I really want to know," Myron said.

Princess sighed and said, "Remember a TV show in the fifties called *Father Knows Best?*"

"I think I've seen reruns," Myron said.

"Well, the father who knew best called his oldest daughter Princess. My father was buggy for that show. I guess he figured that it was good training for us to think that he always knew what he was doing."

"You were named after a character in a TV show?"

"Yeah, but it could have been worse. The youngest daughter was called Kitten."

Myron thought about that as he chewed. How could parents do stuff like that to their own children? Myron said, "I was named after a grandmother in Latvia."

With some surprise, Princess said, "You had a grandmother named Myron?"

"Maybe not Myron. But Miriam or Marsha or Malka or Molly or Marla—one of those *M* names. It's a tradition. I wish I was named James, like your uncle. What's his last name?"

"He's James Grinley, and he's one of the fogies on the board." She threw her arms wide as if she were an actor and declaimed, "Mr. James Grinley, Fogey for Hire." Myron decided that Princess wasn't such a porker once you got to know her. He had a burger in one hand, so, to show his approval, he beat the flat of his hand against the control panel before him. By accident, his hand hit one of the buttons.

48

Suddenly, a great whooping noise began. "What's that?" he shouted over the noise.

"You hit the Intruder Alert button," Princess cried. "Let's get out of here!" She grabbed the remains of her sandwich and the bag it came in and Myron grabbed his own. They leaped down the ladder. The ramp sounded like a big gong beneath their feet as they ran down it. The whooping was very loud in the hangar.

They dived into the round hole in the floor, and Princess pulled the cover back. They stood there on the ladder, listening to the whooping. Suddenly it stopped. Princess whispered, "We got out just in time. Somebody has to be inside to turn off the alarm."

Myron stood beneath her on the ladder, listening to the two of them breathe. He imagined he could hear running footsteps above him, and maybe he could. After a while, Princess said, "I think we can go now." Myron climbed down the ladder.

As they walked back to more civilized parts of the Astronetics building, Princess began to laugh. "That was great! They'll never figure out who was in there! It'll drive them crazy!"

"Yeah," said Myron, though without enthusiasm. He didn't know if he liked the fact that the Tea Cup hangar was quite so easy to get in and out of. After all, the Tea Cup must be secret for a reason. And if he and Princess could get into the hangar, then real Agents of a Foreign Power could too.

As they rode up in the freight elevator, Princess

suddenly stopped laughing and looked embarrassed. She looked away from Myron. Myron glanced around and said, "What's wrong?"

"Nothing," said Princess, but it was clear to Myron that something *was* wrong. Then she said softly, "I never had so much fun with a boy before."

"Uh, thanks." What else could he say? She obviously meant the statement as a compliment.

Princess went on. "I was just wondering if I could come over some night. We could hack around and I could meet your uncle Hugo. He used to be the most interesting guy at Astronetics, but he doesn't come around much anymore."

Myron looked at her in shock. He said, "I dunno. I'd have to ask. Besides, I never invited a girl over for anything before."

"It wouldn't mean we were engaged or anything," Princess said quickly. "You just seem like a good guy."

"Well," said Myron. "I guess you seem like a good guy too. I'll ask Uncle Hugo this evening." Here was another thing he wouldn't be putting into his letter to Arthur.

After they got back to the messenger room, Myron followed Princess around some more. A couple of times they saw a group of men wearing uniforms and silver helmets searching the halls and rooms and offices, looking very serious. Myron and Princess tried to stay out of their way.

Myron and Princess did not speak of their Tea Cup

adventure, even between themselves, but every once in a while one of them would look at the other and they would laugh. Myron couldn't help it. Running around with Princess was fun. He hoped that liking girls was not another part of the Duberville curse.

Late in the afternoon, when they came back to the messenger room, a folded note was on the table. It was for Myron, and it asked him to come visit Mr. Grinley. "I wonder what Uncle James wants," Princess said. She led him to Mr. Grinley's office but would not go in. "Uncle is funny that way. If the invitation were for me too, he would have mentioned my name."

Myron nodded and knocked on the door. "Come in," Mr. Grinley called. Myron took one last look at Princess and went in.

Mr. Grinley's office was even bigger than Mr. Lombardi's. Paintings—not posters—of Astronetics airplanes hung on the walls. Among them were framed things that looked like diplomas. The print was either too small or too fancy for Myron to read without being terribly obvious.

Myron noticed two things about Mr. Grinley right away. The first was that he was one of the two men— the one with the mustache and glasses—who had been talking to Uncle Hugo the day before. He was still wearing a gray suit. The guy must have a whole closet full of them; he wouldn't be the kind of guy who wore the same suit two days in a row.

The second thing Myron noticed was that there was

a family resemblance between Mr. Grinley and Princess. That was what had seemed so familiar about Princess when Myron had first met her. She looked like a miniature Grinley, but without the mustache. Myron wondered whether he looked like a miniature Uncle Hugo.

Mr. Grinley was much more pleased to see Myron than he had been the day before. He rushed around the desk with his hand extended, shook Myron's hand energetically, and offered him a chair. A box of cigars was on Mr. Grinley's desk. Myron almost expected Mr. Grinley to offer him one, but it never happened.

"Well," said Mr. Grinley when they were both settled, "how are we doing? Princess showing you around okay?"

"I'm fine, Mr. Grinley."

"You know, Myron, you strike me as a bright boy. You have the best interests of Astronetics at heart and can recognize those interests if you see them. Isn't that right?" Mr. Grinley smiled. Myron had seen used-car salesmen on TV smile the same way.

Myron said, "I guess so."

Mr. Grinley began to tell him about his Master Plan for Astronetics. Unlike Uncle Hugo, Mr. Grinley wanted to run Astronetics along "sound engineering lines." Grinley and the other board members were not the old fogies that Hugo would like to picture. After all, Astronetics did have a Research and Development Department. "But," said Mr. Grinley, "we try not to let them go off the deep end. Experimentation costs money, and we are in business to make a profit."

Myron had to agree with that. Mr. Grinley certainly sounded as if he were a businessman who knew what he was doing. Next to him, Uncle Hugo seemed like more of a wacko than ever. Myron briefly wondered if every new messenger got this kind of lecture from Mr. Grinley.

Mr. Grinley went on to explain that the Marketing Department had plotted out the direction the R & D Department should go during the next ten years. They had done studies, taken polls, and statistically plotted out exactly what should happen. "You probably have guessed that your uncle's scheme to import titanium from outer space is not part of the Master Plan."

"Yeah, I can see that," said Myron.

"And so," said Mr. Grinley, "I hope that you will accompany your mother to the next stockholders' meeting and tell everyone your experiences with your uncle Hugo."

Myron looked into his lap. Could he agree to this? Uncle Hugo was not a bad guy, for a wacko, anyway. Should Myron's first loyalty be to the family or to the company? Or were they both, in reality, the same thing?

In a different tone, Mr. Grinley said, "Perhaps one more fact will help you make up your mind. Someone was in the Tea Cup this afternoon. They left behind breadcrumbs...," he referred to a folder on his desk, "...bits of hamburger and..."—Mr. Grinley smiled and closed the folder—"...a spot of catsup with a rather clear thumbprint in it."

"Tea Cup?" said Myron. His voice squeaked.

Mr. Grinley nodded slowly. He folded his hands on top of the folder and waited.

Myron was confused. If he was going to make a decision that would radically alter his uncle's life, he wanted it to be the right one. He said carefully, "What about Uncle Hugo?"

"He will be given a generous pension. After that, he can hunt for junk all he wants without embarrassing Astronetics."

"That would be good," said Myron.

Mr. Grinley stood up and said, "I knew you'd see things our way." Myron stood up too. Mr. Grinley put his arm around Myron's shoulder and guided him toward the door. "I'm glad we had this little talk. Thanks for coming in."

Without quite knowing how it had happened, Myron was suddenly in the hallway. Compared to Mr. Grinley, Mr. Lombardi was an amateur at getting people out of his office.

Myron did a lot of thinking while he slowly walked back to the messenger room. He knew that Mr. Grinley was right about running Astronetics along "sound engineering lines," but he was glad that he hadn't made

Mr. Grinley any promises. For all that Mr. Grinley seemed to be a better businessman than Uncle Hugo, his uncle was a nicer person.

Mr. Grinley also thought that Myron had to be threatened before he would do the right thing. Myron didn't like that. He liked to be trusted. Then he wondered how much time he could spend in jail for eating his lunch in the Tea Cup.

Myron thought about the whatsit he'd gotten from the elevator repairman that morning. It somehow represented his entire problem.

When he got back to the messenger room, Princess said, "How'd the meeting go?"

"Oh, okay. Your uncle wanted to talk about my uncle."

"I didn't know Uncle James had an interest in junk."

Myron glared at her.

But Princess said, "Junk is a fact of your life, Myron. No point being shy about it."

Princess was right. Myron had to do something about the junk in his life. He decided that he would do the right thing despite his dislike for Mr. Grinley. He took the whatsit out of his briefcase and threw it into the trash can. It banged against the metal side.

"What was that?" said Princess.

"Just some junk I don't need anymore," said Myron.

He sat at the table thinking glum thoughts and staring at the trash can while Princess collected her coat and the book she'd been reading. He mumbled "good night" when she left for the day.

The longer he sat there, the more it seemed to Myron that throwing away the whatsit had been a mistake. It was too final. It meant that Myron intended to cooperate with Mr. Grinley, and he wasn't certain he was ready to do that. Not yet.

Shaking his head at his own lack of resolve, Myron got up and took the whatsit from the trash can; he put it into the secret compartment of his wallet so it wouldn't tear his pants, and angrily stuffed it into his pocket.

"Maybe *dithering* is the curse of the Dubervilles," he said as he flicked off the lights and strode out of the room.

CHAPTER SIX
CLOSE THE PATENT OFFICE!

Princess was gone. Her father had already come by to pick her up. Too late it occurred to Myron that he could have asked her for a ride home. Now he had a long bus ride ahead of him, and he was not looking forward to it. He was weary after a hard day of trying to get used to new people and a new routine. Thinking about Mr. Grinley and Uncle Hugo made him even more tired.

Myron dawdled down the stairs, thinking these dark thoughts. He said "good night" to the guard now sitting in the receptionist's chair, and walked across the lobby to look out through the great glass double doors. Parked right out front was Uncle Hugo's junk truck.

"Want a ride?" said a voice behind him.

Myron turned to see Uncle Hugo sitting on a couch, just putting down a copy of *Big Bucks* magazine. He smiled at Myron. It was a real smile, not the kind that Mr. Grinley used. Myron weighed his desire to ride home with Uncle Hugo against his desire not to be seen in the junk truck. Boy, was he tired. He smiled back at Uncle Hugo and said, "I guess."

Myron slouched down in the cab of the truck, willing himself invisible. Uncle Hugo started the truck with a roar, and they bounced off. As his uncle drove, glancing occasionally into the rearview mirror, he told Myron about the busy day he'd had. Each piece of junk in the truck bed had its story. Once, Uncle Hugo said, "Saw a strange woman today too."

"Oh?" said Myron.

"Yes. Black woman in a white nineteen sixty Chevrolet Belvedere just like mine. She seemed very interested in my activities."

"Did you talk to her?"

"No. Should I have?"

"I guess not. Except that I saw her yesterday, when you drove me home from the airport."

"Really? What was she doing?"

"Mostly, she was just watching you. But she seemed awfully friendly with the light pole she ran into." Should he have said that? It was certain to feed Uncle Hugo's fantasies.

"That so? If I see her again, I guess I will talk to her. What kind of day did *you* have?"

He had had a rotten day, but there seemed no point

in telling Uncle Hugo about it. Brightly, Myron said, "You were right. It looks like Astronetics is a real successful company."

Uncle Hugo nodded. As he spoke, he glanced into his rearview mirror again. "Mostly your father's doing. If it hadn't been for him, I'd still be fixing airplanes in Joplin, Missouri."

Myron looked up from his slouch and said, "Is there something wrong?"

"Wrong?"

"You keep looking into your rearview mirror."

Uncle Hugo laughed. He said, "Take a look out the back window."

Myron tried to smile. It was not entirely a success. He turned around in his seat and stood on his knees as he looked out the window at the back of the cab. He had a good view of traffic and that day's junk. "I don't see anything in particular," Myron said.

"Watch this," said Uncle Hugo. He signaled and drove one lane to the left. Then he signaled again and this time drove one lane to the right. "See anything unusual?" he asked.

"Every time you changed lanes, a big old car behind us changed lanes too."

Uncle Hugo laughed again and said, "That's Grinley's hired bloodhound."

"You mean that Mr. Grinley has hired somebody to follow you?"

"Pretty strange, huh? He's hired a detective to follow me and gather evidence to prove I'm crazy. The detective is named Art Poindexter and he wears a fedora and trench coat just like Bogart did in all his detective movies."

Myron could just make out the guy who was driving. He did seem to be wearing a hat of some kind. A cigarette drooped from the middle of his intense expression. "Aren't you worried that Mr. Poindexter will report to Mr. Grinley about your truck?"

"I'm not worried about Mr. Poindexter at all. A detective who needs to wear a uniform to convince himself he *is* a detective can't be very dangerous. The cheaper the detective, the gaudier the clothing. Besides, as you must know by now, the truck is not a secret."

Myron turned around and sat in his seat again. Maybe Aspen was too close. Maybe he should hitchhike to South America to see if he could find his father.

"Thinking?" asked Uncle Hugo.

"I have a question I'd like to ask you, and I really need to have the absolute most honest answer you can give me. But I won't ask it if it'll make you angry."

"Be brave," Uncle Hugo said.

"You got angry when I asked you if you were spending Astronetics money on junk."

"I got angry at your tone, not at your question. Anyone has a right to ask questions. No one has a right to be impolite."

Myron looked at his feet. He said, "I'm sorry about

the tone, Uncle Hugo." He went on, watching his uncle's face for signs of anger. "I guess I was a little excited, hearing for the first time about..." Myron tried to think of the least offensive way to say what he had been excited about. "...about your problem with Mr. Grinley and Mr. Pinch."

"Your excitement is perfectly understandable, my boy." Uncle Hugo shrugged as if unloading the whole topic. "It's no secret I'm spending Astronetics money on junk. What Grinley and Pinch fail to understand is that Astronetics stands to make a lot *more* money when the titanium begins to arrive."

"Uh-huh. Okay. My question is this. Uncle Hugo, *are* you crazy?"

Uncle Hugo glanced at Myron and said, "You've been talking to Grinley, haven't you?"

"More like he's been talking to me."

"And he's been telling you about how he wants to run Astronetics along 'sound engineering lines.'"

"He seems to know what he's doing," Myron said quietly.

"He's a hard-headed businessman, all right. He'd do just fine if he were selling soap or corn flakes. But..." Uncle Hugo shook his head. He smiled a sad, whimsical smile. "Well, we'll talk more at the house."

Osgood met them at the front door. "What's for dinner?" asked Uncle Hugo.

"Meat loaf, as you requested, sir."

"Don't hide the catsup this time," Uncle Hugo said as he slipped past Osgood into the house.

"Evening, Osgood," said Myron.

"Good evening, Master Duberville."

Myron followed his uncle into the library. "Close the door," said Uncle Hugo. Myron did.

Uncle Hugo began pulling photographs and newspaper clippings from a drawer and throwing them on his desk. "Have a look at this, Myron. And this and this. . . ."

Myron picked up a photograph of the X-15, the first American ship in space, and a photograph of Neil Armstrong on the moon. There were newspaper clippings about microchips and space shuttles and communications satellites. "Wow," said Myron, "an autographed picture of Chuck Yeager, the test pilot!"

Uncle Hugo said, "Astronetics had something to do with every one of these projects."

"Wow," Myron said again. He sat down in the chair, still holding the Yeager photo.

"Put the picture on the desk, Myron," said Uncle Hugo gently.

When Myron had done so, Uncle Hugo said, "None of this would have happened if we followed Grinley's 'sound engineering lines.' We'd still have radios with tubes and airplanes with propellers."

"He must be right about some things," Myron said.

"Maybe. If the future of science and engineering is

predictable, then he is right. If we will find things we didn't expect, which is more likely, then he is wrong." Uncle Hugo picked up a sheet of paper and said, "Try to guess who made these statements, and when." Without waiting for Myron to answer, he went on: " 'There is no likelihood man can ever tap the power of the atom.' " He looked at Myron.

Myron said, "I don't know."

"It was Robert Millikan, who won the Nobel Prize for Physics in nineteen twenty-three. Thirty-two years later, the atomic submarine *Nautilus* was launched."

"Hm," said Myron.

"And this: 'Heavier-than-air flying machines are impossible.' "

"Mr. Grinley?"

"Might as well have been," said Uncle Hugo. "In reality, it was Lord Kelvin, president of the British Royal Society of Science in about eighteen ninety-five, or eight years before the Wright Brothers flew at Kitty Hawk. One more: 'Everything that can be invented has been invented.' "

Myron shook his head.

"It was a dunderhead named Charles H. Duell, who was the director of the United States Patent Office in eighteen ninety-nine."

Myron said, "But some of these guys must have been right sometime."

"Of course they were. The point is that nobody is

right all the time, least of all about the future. Grinley is less likely to be right because the 'sound engineering lines of today' tend to be the quaint curiosities of tomorrow. Get me?" Uncle Hugo began to push his photos and clippings together into a neat pile.

Myron nodded. Maybe Uncle Hugo wasn't such a wacko—especially compared to Mr. Grinley. Myron wished he hadn't had lunch with Princess in the Tea Cup. That made it difficult to ignore Mr. Grinley, even if Myron thought he was wrong.

With an almost physical effort, Myron pushed aside the urge to ask Uncle Hugo for help with Mr. Grinley. It wasn't that he was afraid Uncle Hugo would threaten Myron the way Mr. Grinley had. He just thought it unwise to tell an adult any more about his personal troubles than the adult absolutely needed to know.

"I hope that's cleared up where I stand on Grinley's 'sound engineering lines.' Now I have some sorting to do." Uncle Hugo indicated a pile of junk on the floor next to his desk. "I'll see you at dinner."

Myron said, "Okay, Uncle Hugo." When he got to the door, he remembered something and turned back. "Uncle Hugo?"

"Yes, Myron."

"Do you know Mr. Grinley's niece, Princess?"

"Everybody knows Princess," Uncle Hugo said.

"Do you think I could invite her over tonight after dinner?"

"Why not?" Uncle Hugo picked up a crooked potato masher, which he studied with a critical eye. He had forgotten Myron was there. Myron closed the library door.

Myron went up to his room and looked for something that might be a telephone. What kind of telephone did the Skyjacks of the Universe use? In the drawer of the table next to the bed—the bed that was not there at the moment—Myron found the very thing. It looked like two credit cards stuck together face to face.

Myron sat down in one of the molded plastic chairs. A tinny dial tone sounded when he slid the top card back to reveal a touch pad set up like telephone buttons. He slid the card together, and the dial tone stopped.

As he searched through his pockets to find Princess's phone number, he began to sweat. He'd never called a girl before. He didn't know what the two of them would do together once she got to Uncle Hugo's house. It had to be something spectacular if it was going to match their adventure with the Tea Cup. Of course, he didn't have to call her at all. Then, tomorrow, he could tell her he'd lost the number—but that was the coward's way out.

Myron found her number and set it before him on the table. He wiped his sweaty hands on his gray pants and slid the phone open. This time, instead of a dial tone, he heard a voice.

"—the right thing." That had to be the voice of somebody in the house. Every phone in the place was probably tied into the same outside line.

"Don't worry about a thing. This is for the good of The Company."

"I've been with Mr. Duberville for twenty-two years. I'd like to do what's good for *him*, too."

"If you would like to back out, Osgood, I'm sure someone else would enjoy spending the rest of his or her life in Acapulco."

"No, no. Just want to make certain I'm doing the right thing, that's all. No need for talk of backing out. I'll be there about nine."

"Don't be late." The line clicked as the man at the other end hung up. The line clicked again as Osgood hung up.

Myron was astonished. Here was Osgood, obviously about to do something nasty to Uncle Hugo for the sake of "The Company." The Company could only be Astronetics, and Myron was certain the voice at the other end had been Mr. Grinley's. Something underhanded was about to happen. Myron could tell Uncle Hugo, or he could—

Myron smiled. His hands shook as he punched Princess's number into the card. Her father, Mr. Grinley, answered the phone. He sounded like her uncle, Mr. Grinley, but nicer, without the snake oil. Myron knew that when he spoke on the phone, he had no secrets.

He would have to be careful of what he said to Princess.

When she came on the line at last, Myron said, "Princess, come dressed for an adventure."

CHAPTER SEVEN
WIRED FOR SOUND

Myron decided that he had better dress for an adventure himself. He discovered how to make his closet rotate out of the wall and spent a little time trying to decide what he should wear.

While he chose his clothing, he also tried to imagine what Mr. Grinley might think of his having the adventure he was planning. It certainly had nothing to do with any stockholders' meeting. Still, Mr. Grinley might not see this in the same light as Myron did. He might decide that anything Myron did to help Uncle Hugo would be cause enough to tell the Air Force or whomever about his visit to the Tea Cup.

Myron stood for a moment, holding in each hand a golf shirt that had a pelican on the pocket. Helping Uncle Hugo was important. Also, it was important to keep Astronetics out of the clutches of Mr. Grinley and his "sound engineering lines."

Besides, Myron thought, I might not get caught. And if I do get caught, Uncle Hugo might be able to save me from going to federal prison. Furthermore, Myron needed something to do with Princess that evening. Nothing else seemed to fit the bill.

Myron became aware that he was holding the golf shirts. He wanted to wear one of them, but they were both pretty colorful and didn't seem right for sneaking around in. He finally decided to wear a black T-shirt that had the words A. CLARKSON SCHOOL OF BUSINESS ADMINISTRATION on the chest in white letters. He also changed into a pair of nearly new designer jeans that he sometimes wore (the back pocket had a little penguin stitched on it) and his Ready Fox jogging shoes.

Uncle Hugo nodded at Myron when they met at the dinner table. The checkered tablecloth was now blue instead of red. Myron enjoyed dinner, though he was so excited about Princess's upcoming visit, he thought the meal would never end. Osgood made a good meat loaf, with plenty of bits of onion in it, and, as ordered, he had not hidden the catsup. Uncle Hugo complained that the broccoli was too crisp, though Myron thought it was very soggy indeed.

After dinner, he went back up to his room, hoping that he could learn to run it before Princess arrived and he embarrassed himself in front of her. Making the bed roll in and out of the wall was easy. He'd seen Osgood—the traitor!—do that. But Myron was surprised to see that some machine inside the wall had made up the bed with clean linen. He approved.

He'd learned how to turn the lights in the walls up or down. He'd had to, or he'd have gotten no sleep the night before. And learning how to run the bathroom the night before also had seemed like a good idea. The workings of the green-tiled room were a series of puzzles concocted by a demon plumber; everything was hidden in the wall, and when you found a pipe or a spigot or a pressure switch, it rarely did what you expected it to do. Myron had gotten plenty wet in the process. He thought he understood the fixtures now, but he would not be surprised if they turned on him again.

He found that by raising his hand to various heights over various surfaces, he could bring forth or take away more furniture, a drinking fountain, a fully programmed computer terminal (complete with encyclopedia, phone directory, dictionary, thesaurus, atlas, star charts, and the complete *Skyjacks of the Universe* script), potted palms, a bird cage complete with parakeet, and lots more stuff, most of which he had no use for.

If he moved his hand just the right distance in front of the empty spaces in the walls that looked like blank TV screens, they became what seemed to be windows that looked out over the backyard. If he stood close enough, he could see by the wavy lines that made up the pictures that the windows really *were* big TV screens. Everything had a tag or a label on it somewhere that said it came from the Catalog of Raunchypur, and that removing the tag or label was an interstellar offense punishable to the full extent of the law.

While Myron was still working up nerve to mess with a line of glowing cubes and other controls he had found behind a wall panel, the entire house began to shake. "Earthquake!" he yelled, and ran to crouch in a doorway because he had once read that a doorway was the safest place to stand during an earthquake. He waited for the worst to happen.

A rumbling grew in intensity until it sounded as if Niagara Falls were right there in his bedroom with him. Then, suddenly, the sound and the shaking were gone. Seconds later, while Myron was still catching his breath, he heard Osgood's voice over an intercom he hadn't even known was there. Osgood said, "Your guest is here, Master Duberville."

"Thanks, Osgood," Myron cried, and ran downstairs.

Princess, Uncle Hugo, and Osgood were in the front hall. Uncle Hugo was just saying, "I'm delighted to see you, Princess."

Princess was decked out in clothes made entirely of denim. Her black boots had buckles all over them, even in places where they didn't seem to be actually holding anything together. There was no animal on the pocket of her denim jacket, but across the chest of her maroon T-shirt it said TOXIC SOX, which Myron kind of

71

liked, despite himself. She was dressed for adventure, all right.

"Uh, thanks," was all Princess said. She used a finger to brush her bangs from the top of her glasses and gawked at all the spaceships suspended from the ceiling and the robot stained-glass window and the paintings of all the movie and television aliens. Myron was surprised to see her act so shy.

She smiled with relief when she saw Myron, but before he even said hello to her, he cried, "Osgood, what was that noise?"

"You are referring to the rumbling and whooshing, sir?"

"What else would I be referring to?"

"I could not say, sir. However, the rumbling and whooshing is the front doorbell. Your uncle thought that it would be interesting if it sounded like a spaceship blasting off." He looked gloomily, as usual, at Uncle Hugo.

"Pretty spectacular, isn't it Myron?" Uncle Hugo said. Myron agreed that it was.

Uncle Hugo said he had to get back into the library because he had lots of sorting to do yet. He turned to Princess and said, "Please come and see us again soon."

Princess smiled nervously but said nothing.

When his uncle was gone, Myron said, "Hi, Princess."

"Hi, yourself." Princess seemed to be her old self again. "This is some great place your uncle has here."

72

"Pretty weird, huh?" said Myron. He noticed Osgood hanging around, pretending to be dusting a painting of some alien who had an enormous head and eyes like pine cones.

"Some kids would probably pay you big money to visit this place. How many of these ships can *you* identify?"

"Uh, a few," said Myron while he watched Osgood. "I have to get my sweater. You want to come with me and see my room? It's pretty strange."

Princess followed Myron up the stairs. Myron opened the outside door of his room the regular way you open a door, then opened the *Skyjacks* door with the blue printlock. When they got inside, Princess recognized the room right away. Because she knew *Skyjacks of the Universe* so well, she could even show Myron tricks he had not yet learned. She twisted one of the glowing cubes that Myron had discovered after dinner and made the ceiling transparent. With a slider, she rotated a rack out of the wall. The rack held ten blasters.

Princess took a blaster from the rack and began to wave it around. She moved with more grace than Myron would have expected a girl of her size to possess. She turned suddenly and pointed the blaster at a chair. "Look out, Captain!" she cried, and made a warbling sound with her mouth. "Too bad they're not real," she said, and threw the blaster on a chair. Myron put it away.

Meanwhile Princess continued to experiment with the cube controls. She looked around as if waiting for something to happen and said, "What, no antigravity?"

"We're having it installed tomorrow." They both laughed at this as if they were little kids.

When they were done laughing, Princess said, "So, what is this adventure you were talking about?"

Hoping that she had not said too much already, Myron put his finger to his lips and ran his hand in a complicated pattern over a section of blank wall. In a way that his eye could not quite follow, a desk unfolded from the wall, and a chair rolled toward him out of the knee hole. He sat down, found a pad of paper in one tof the drawers, and wrote, *We can't talk here. Let's go for a walk outside.*

Princess nodded and, as if she were an actress, said, "You want to show me the grounds?" "Sure," Myron said. He grabbed a chocolate-brown sweater that had a chorus line of deer prancing across the chest, and they closed up the room and went outside.

It was still light when they crossed the backyard, but the sun was definitely going down and it would be dark soon. A cool wind blew through the trees, shaking the leaves. Myron buttoned his deer sweater and Princess zipped up her denim jacket halfway. "Won't you still be cold?" said Myron.

"Sometimes," said Princess, "looking cool is more

important than being warm. What are we doing out here?"

"We can't talk in my room. I think the entire house is wired for sound."

"With a techno-freak like your uncle, you have to expect stuff like that."

"Yeah, but I don't have to like it. Anyway, I have something to tell you that I don't want anybody else to know, particularly not ol' Osgood."

Princess nodded.

When he told her what he'd heard on the phone, her eyes got wide behind her glasses. She and Myron came to the gravel road, and without even noticing, they began to walk along it toward the barn. Myron looked at his watch. "Osgood said he had to be wherever by nine. It's seven twenty-three now—"

"Seven twenty-five," Princess said.

"Twenty-three," Myron said. He shoved his wristwatch into her face. Then she shoved her wristwatch into his face.

They kept up this argument so long that after a while, Myron was saying seven twenty-four and Princess was saying seven twenty-six. Myron no longer cared who was right. He was arguing for the honor of his Benelux wristwatch.

Suddenly, Princess stopped hollering numbers in the high twenties and said, sort of breathlessly, "What's that?"

In the gathering darkness, what she pointed to could have been a hayrick or the top of a buried giant. "It's a junk heap," Myron said.

"What's it doing here?"

"I don't know. I suppose it's more of Uncle Hugo's aliens."

"Aliens? You mean like refugees from El Salvador or—"

"Not El Salvador," said Myron. He told her Uncle Hugo's idea about sending aliens back to their own planet in exchange for ships full of titanium.

"Oh yeah? How will he send them back?"

"He has a specially modified nineteen sixty Chevrolet Belvedere." Myron pointed in the direction of the barn, which neither of them could see in the dark.

"I have to see this," said Princess.

Myron told her Uncle Hugo kept the barn locked, but she wanted to see it anyway. They walked to the end of the gravel road; then Myron stood in front of the barn while Princess walked all the way around it.

When she stood beside him again, she said, "Your Uncle Hugo is in big trouble."

Myron nodded. "Yeah. And I think that Osgood visiting your uncle, Mr. Grinley, won't help."

"Makes sense."

"Do you want to help me?" Myron asked.

"Help you what?"

"Well," Myron said slowly. Now that the moment

had come when they were to begin their adventure, Myron was not sure that he wanted Princess in on it. He said, "I don't know. You're Mr. Grinley's niece."

"So?" Princess looked at a point somewhere near the roof of the barn.

Myron, his thoughts dithering again—*The Return of the Curse of the Dubervilles*—didn't say anything.

"Well, then don't tell me," Princess said, and folded her arms.

"All right. I won't." Myron marched off, back down the gravel road. He knew that he had made the right decision. Princess could not tell her uncle what she didn't know.

"Where are you going?" Princess called after him.

"I'm going to do what I was going to do, only now I'm going to do it alone."

Princess ran to catch up with him, then matched him stride for stride. He pretended she wasn't there. Princess said, "If you don't let me help, I *will* tell."

Myron laughed. "Don't let me stop you. Your uncle already knows everything I just told you." He walked a little faster.

Princess didn't say anything for a while, but she kept right up. When they walked past the pile of junk, Princess said, "He doesn't know that you know about Osgood."

Myron kept walking while he tried to decide if what Princess had just said was important. He felt cornered again. Myron had visions of rotating Princess behind a wall in his room, feeding her rolled-up slices of baloney through the keyhole, and keeping her there till somehow he'd gotten out from under Mr. Grinley and made sure that Uncle Hugo had permanent control over Astronetics.

Myron couldn't do that, of course. For one thing, somebody was sure to miss a girl like Princess, and her trail would eventually lead to him. Men would be hired to tear down his room with crowbars. She would be found and she would tell all. Not only would Uncle Hugo lose Astronetics, but Myron would go to jail.

Murder seemed attractive for just a fleeting second.

"All right," Myron said. "Come on."

CHAPTER EIGHT
THE HAND OF FIRE

Myron didn't know if Princess was a spy for Mr. Grinley, but he did know that he was glad to have her with him. She seemed so confident that she gave Myron confidence too. Which was just as well. Under these circumstances, he reflected, even pelicans on his pockets might not have done the trick.

They walked more slowly now and spoke in conspiratorial tones. Myron said, "Did you know that your Uncle Grinley has a detective named Art Poindexter following my uncle Hugo?"

"No, I didn't."

"Well, he does. I figure I can convince Mr. Poindexter that Osgood is going somewhere for Uncle Hugo, and that we ought to see where Osgood is going."

"If Mr. Poindexter works for my uncle James, maybe he already knows where Osgood is going. And why. And everything."

"Well, maybe. On the other hand, your uncle, Mr. Grinley, probably doesn't tell Mr. Poindexter everything."

"No," said Princess. "Telling people things is not Uncle James's style. He certainly didn't tell me about any detective. Where is this Poindexter guy?"

"He's got to be on the grounds somewhere. He's supposed to be watching Uncle Hugo."

"You mean you don't even know where he is?"

Myron didn't like Princess's tone. Rashly, he said, "If you think finding him will be too tough, you can go home now."

"Sorry."

That didn't sound like the feisty Princess he knew. He looked at her to see if she was laughing at him. Miraculously, she was not. Myron said, "I figure we should spread out. The one who finds him comes to tell the other."

"Okay."

"Okay then."

"All right."

"I'll go this way," Myron said. "You look down the road. We'll meet in front of the barn in half an hour."

Princess nodded and walked off. Myron watched her for a few seconds, then set out through a gap in the hedge at the side of the road and was immediately in a thick forest.

The cool air smelled sweet with night-blooming flowers. Myron could see pretty well because there was a quarter moon in the sky. Still, shadows were everywhere. The longer he moved around in them, the more he was convinced that he was not the only one out skulking that night. Of course not. He laughed to himself. Princess and Mr. Poindexter were out there somewhere. He hoped it was just the three of them.

He stopped and held his breath. He listened so hard, his ears began to ring. He heard leaves rustling and branches creaking. He hoped they were leaves and branches. Something flew by quickly on leathery wings.

Sheesh! There were bats out here! Myron knew that there were no such creatures as vampires—people who turned into bats and sucked blood—but the bats bothered him anyway. Who knew what a bat would do if it was hungry?

Myron entered a clearing. In the center of it was a small round house with columns supporting the roof, but no walls. Three steps led up into the creepy house. It was painted white, and it stood out from the forest as if it were enchanted.

Myron circled the house while looking out into the forest. Suddenly, he saw a light moving among the trees. He froze. He not only stopped moving entirely, but he felt cold all over. Of course, that light could belong to Mr. Poindexter. That was logical. Who else would be out here with a flashlight? Princess didn't have one that Myron knew of.

Trying to make as little noise as possible, Myron walked toward the light. He tried to remember all he could from Davy Crockett reruns and Daniel Boone movies about how to move silently through the forest.

The light kept appearing and disappearing as whoever was carrying it walked among the trees. Myron made a big circle and tried to get behind the person. He lost sight of the light. Soon, he was in another clearing. He could tell it was not the same one he had been in before because it had a big stone birdbath in it instead of that strange house without walls.

Myron saw the light behind a tree at the edge of the clearing. It wasn't moving. If the flashlight belonged to Mr. Poindexter, he was obviously looking at something behind the tree, or waiting for something or someone. Could he be waiting for Osgood? Myron didn't know enough about what was going on, that was for sure.

He crept forward on his toes, doing his best impression of a frontiersman. He looked around the tree and saw a sort of hulking blob crouching over an ancient water pump that jutted at an angle from the ground.

Myron said warily, "Mr. Poindexter?"

What happened next was difficult to sort out because it seemed to happen all at once. The hulking blob looked up at Myron. It wasn't Mr. Poindexter. It was that wacko of a woman he'd seen petting the light pole when Uncle Hugo had stopped on the way home from the airport. She thrust her palm at him as if she were trying to push him away. The palm was glowing with a light that was so bright, it blinded him for a moment. The woman screamed and ran.

Myron screamed and ran the other way while balloons of colored light popped before his eyes. He had not run far when he stopped and looked around. He really should be running after the woman so that he could find out what she wanted. But the balloons were still flashing around him. As the lights in his head diminished, the forest looked darker than it had. He could see no light among the trees. He heard nothing that sounded like someone running or walking.

Myron waited what seemed to be a long time, hoping that the woman would start moving again. But he became stiff and bored and finally decided that she was gone for good.

"Myron?"

Myron jumped and turned. Someone was standing before him. He took a step back.

"Myron, it's me. Princess."

"Princess. How'd you sneak up on me like that?"

"Girl Scouts don't just sell cookies, you know."

"Yeah, well don't do it again. Did you find Mr. Poindexter?"

Princess nodded and said, "He's parked out at the end of this gravel road. He's waiting for us in his car." Princess stepped forward and peered into Myron's face. "Gee, you look awful. What's the matter?"

"I saw *her.*"

"Her who?"

"I don't know what her name is, but she seems awfully interested in Uncle Hugo."

Princess looked around. She said, "Maybe Uncle James hired her, too."

"I don't think so. I saw her on the way in from the airport. Besides, I don't think your uncle knows anybody who has a hand that shines in the dark."

Princess said, "You're making that shining-hand stuff up to pay me back for scaring you just now."

"Have it your way."

"You're not making it up?"

"No."

They looked around. The fire balloons were gone, and Myron could see a lot more of the forest now. He knelt, looking for footprints in the moonlight. But the pine-needle carpet showed nothing.

While peering into the dark columns of trees, Princess said, "Then maybe your uncle Hugo is right about aliens visiting the earth."

Myron shook his head. "I'm willing to buy a woman with a hand of fire being an alien, but I'm not ready to believe old bits of junk are from another planet." He stood up and said, "Well, I guess we'd better go. Mr. Poindexter is waiting for us."

"Yeah, and we wouldn't want to miss Osgood."

Myron nodded. Still looking around, they walked off

together. Myron had to admit that Princess could move very quietly.

"Mr. Poindexter wasn't too happy to see me," Princess said.

"Why not? As far as he's concerned, you're just some kid."

"Just some kid who was told by your uncle Hugo that a detective was following him."

"Oops," said Myron eloquently.

"Yeah," said Princess. "Oops. How else would we know that Mr. Poindexter existed?"

Myron sighed. He said, "So, what's he going to do?"

"Nothing yet. When I left him, he was still thinking."

"Then we're really in trouble. The detectives on TV are always good thinkers."

"Yeah, well, so far the only thing Mr. Poindexter is good at is quoting lines from *The Maltese Falcon* and *The Big Sleep*. He must have seen the movies. Something tells me he's not the type that reads books."

The car was so ancient, Myron had never heard of it. Glinting in the moonlight, metal letters on its side said HUDSON. Myron was used to modern compact cars, so the inside of the Hudson looked huge, like the inside of a big padded cave. Mr. Poindexter was sitting behind the wheel, still wearing his trench coat and fedora, grabbing shelled peanuts from a big striped bag and popping them into his mouth. A cigarette was burning in a tiny ceramic toilet that was taped to the dashboard.

Princess slid into the middle of the front seat next to Mr. Poindexter, and Myron sat next to the window. The whole car smelled of cigarette smoke and peanuts.

"Here's looking at *you,* kids," said Mr. Poindexter, and laughed. The laugh soon turned into a cough and he took a puff on his cigarette. Myron waited for Mr. Poindexter to offer him and Princess peanuts, but he never did. "So," said Mr. Poindexter, "you kids want to be detectives."

"Sure," said Myron, uncertain about what Princess had been telling him. "We figure tailing Osgood will be good practice."

"Besides," said Princess, "we like doing Uncle James, that is, Mr. Grinley, favors."

"Anything you say, sweetheart," Mr. Poindexter said. Only when he said "sweetheart," it sounded like "schweetheart." His lips twitched. Then he popped more peanuts into his mouth and, while he chewed them, glanced at the kids as if making sure they were watching his performance.

Myron tried not to laugh when Princess turned to him and made her lips twitch as Poindexter's had. Princess was right. Poindexter probably wasn't much of a detective if he thought he had to go around imitating Humphrey Bogart.

"I don't know why I shouldn't tell Mr. Grinley that you kids want to follow Osgood. You're taking the fall, sweethearts." He appraised them as if waiting for them to buy him off with a bag of peanuts.

Myron said, "I know why."

"I'm waiting," Mr. Poindexter said.

"Because," said Myron, "if you tell Mr. Grinley that we wanted to follow Osgood, he'll ask us how *we* knew about *you*. And we'll be forced to tell him."

Princess said, "How happy do you think Mr. Grinley will be to know that we heard about you from Hugo Duberville, the man you are supposed to be following? Sweetheart."

Mr. Poindexter shook a finger at Princess and said, "I was just going to say that." He took his cigarette from the little ceramic toilet and puffed on it for a while. Myron opened the window. The air that came into the car was cold, but at least it was relatively clean.

Mr. Poindexter seemed to come to a decision. He nodded and said, "You kids are good. Yes you are." Evidently, this meant that as far as he was concerned, the incident was over. He launched into a long story about his experiences. That's what he called them, experiences.

He talked about his involvement in a search for a statue of a black bird covered with jewels, about his search for a thin man, and the mystery of the Hound of the Bubermans.

As if she were sharing a joke, Princess said, "I've seen those movies too."

Mr. Poindexter stopped chewing and leveled a scowl at Princess that should have caused her to evaporate. Then he said. "I won't play the sap for you, sweetheart. You keep cracking wise, and Osgood can chase himself."

"Tell us more, Mr. Poindexter," Myron said.

Mr. Poindexter relaxed. As he talked, Myron got colder and stared out the windshield of the Hudson. The view was not exactly interesting. It was so quiet and still that Myron might have been looking out the window at a big photograph. All he could see was the end of the driveway that swept up to Uncle Hugo's mansion. There was a street lamp right across the street. Myron thought he could see bugs flitting around the light.

If the street hadn't been paved, and there hadn't been a street lamp, all the trees and bushes and stuff would make this place seem as if it were in the middle of nowhere, he thought. Of course, without the street lamp, he would have been able to see very little. Cripes, my mind is running around in circles. Maybe I'm tired. Maybe I ought to go to bed. Who cares where Osgood goes, anyway?

Myron looked at Princess for a clue as to how she felt, but she was evidently enthralled by Mr. Poindexter's latest experience. Mr. Poindexter was talking about how he had once tailed a man for three weeks just to find out what color his underwear was. Myron waited impatiently for Mr. Poindexter to finish. When he did, Myron said, "Mr. Poindexter, do you know anything about Mr. Grinley hiring some woman to watch Uncle Hugo?"

"He's hired some woman?" Mr. Poindexter sounded more worried than surprised.

Myron shrugged. "I don't know. But there was a strange woman out on the grounds tonight." Myron thought that a man like Mr. Poindexter might not understand a woman whose hands glowed in the dark, so he left that part out.

"Her hands glowed in the dark," Princess said.

"You're good, sweetheart. You're really good." Mr. Poindexter nodded and winked.

"Myron told me all about her. I didn't see her myself."

Princess and Mr. Poindexter looked at Myron. It was quiet enough in the Hudson for Myron to hear Mr. Poindexter's rusty breathing.

At last Myron said, "I don't know who she was or anything. Some kind of wacko, probably."

"Yeah," Mr. Poindexter said. "The world is full of wackos. Or maybe it was one of your uncle's aliens." He laughed and coughed and smoked his cigarette. Myron thought the whole production was pretty disgusting. He noticed that Princess's shoulder was tight against his. Myron didn't think it was because Princess was a big girl, or because she had any particular fondness for him. The front seat was large, but she could move only so far away from Mr. Poindexter.

After that, they just sat and waited. According to Myron's Benelux watch, it was nearly eight thirty. Osgood ought to be starting out pretty soon.

And sure enough, it was not many minutes later when they heard the sound of an automobile coming down the driveway. They watched as a small boxy Japanese car stopped at the end of the driveway and then turned and shot down the street.

"Here we go," said Mr. Poindexter as he started the Hudson's engine. Seconds later they were booming down the street after Osgood.

CHAPTER NINE
A PROFESSIONAL HUNCH

The Hudson followed the Japanese car through the nighttime streets of Vasichvu Bend. They headed down the hill and toward the center of town. Myron remembered how easily he had spotted Mr. Poindexter from the junk truck earlier that day, and he wondered if Osgood would notice the Hudson behind him. Well, Osgood was not expecting to be followed. It was night. Everything helped.

Still, Mr. Poindexter managed to lose Osgood at a red light. Mr. Poindexter swore under his breath, using words that Myron had not often heard and had never used himself. When the light turned green, the Japanese car was nowhere in sight.

"What do we do now?" Myron said as Mr. Poindexter pulled over to the curb. The engine chugged while the detective thought.

Myron was restless. Each minute, Osgood was getting farther away and more difficult to follow. If they didn't catch him, they might never find out what he and Mr. Grinley were plotting against Uncle Hugo.

Mr. Poindexter bit his lip. "Uh," he said, "I have a hunch."

"A hunch?" Princess said as if she did not believe in such things.

Mr. Poindexter glared at Princess and said, "I'm a professional, sweetheart. Hunches are part of the business. Ain't you never seen *The Big Sleep?*"

"Seen it *and* read it," Myron said.

"There's a book?" Mr. Poindexter said as he edged the Hudson into the traffic and then raced off.

Myron was developing a hunch himself. It tickled the back of his mind, bothered him in a fleeting way. But he was not a professional detective so he did not trust the hunch. Myron only nudged Princess with his elbow and smiled at her with a reassurance he did not feel. Princess said, "Why not check it out? All we're burning is gasoline, I suppose."

Pretty soon they passed a big neon sign that said CIPHER CITY—NOTHING IS LIKE IT. They drove among tall office buildings that looked like ocean liners standing on end, and fancy restaurants that had crowds of well-dressed people standing around outside.

"What are we doing here?" Myron asked.

"Osgood's in Cipher City someplace," the detective answered.

Myron could see that Princess was about to say something, but she never got a chance because Mr. Poindexter suddenly swung the Hudson into an underground parking garage. "There he is," Mr. Poindexter cried.

"Where?" Myron and Princess cried together.

"You two got blinders on?" Mr. Poindexter pointed at one of the few cars parked in the garage. It looked like Osgood's, but so did a lot of cars. Mr. Poindexter pulled the Hudson up next to it.

"How did you see his car from out on the street?" Princess said.

"Talent, sweetheart," Mr. Poindexter said. "Come on." He rolled out of the car, heavy and clumsy as a bear. Princess and Myron did not move.

Myron's hunch had turned out to be correct. He called out the open door, "I think we want to go home."

"Home?" Mr. Poindexter said. "We just got here."

Princess said, "You know an awful lot for a man working on hunches."

Mr. Poindexter thrust his hand into his trench coat pocket and suddenly a bulge was pointed at Myron and Princess. Mr. Poindexter said, "I got a little friend in my pocket. He wants you to get out of the car."

"Do you think he has a gun?" Myron whispered.

"Do you want to find out the hard way?" Princess whispered back.

Myron and Princess got out of the car. "All right, sweethearts," Mr. Poindexter said gently, "this way."

He pushed them before him and guided them to an elevator. Over the elevator it said WELCOME TO THE MAGNIFICENT RAFF BUILDING. The detective pushed the UP button.

"Where are you taking us?" Myron said.

"You'll see, sweetheart. You're going over. You're taking the fall."

Princess said, "Do you know how silly you sound when you talk like some old detective movie?"

Mr. Poindexter prodded Princess with the bulge in his trench-coat pocket and said, "Can the lip, sister."

"If you're taking us to see Mr. Grinley," Myron said, "you're making a big mistake. We'll tell him that my uncle Hugo knows all about you."

The elevator arrived and Mr. Poindexter pushed Myron and Princess aboard. He crowded them against the back wall and pushed the 17 button. As the elevator rose, he stood with his back to the door, still covering them with the bulge in his trench coat.

"You're smart, angel, but not too smart. Mr. Grinley already knows that your uncle Hugo knows that I'm following him. Mr. Grinley also knows that your uncle Hugo couldn't care less."

Myron shook his head and said, "I should have known it was too easy to convince you to follow Osgood."

Princess said, "We walked right into his trap." She sounded disgusted with herself.

"You did?" said Mr. Poindexter in happy surprise.

"Yeah, you did! And I think Mr. Grinley will be real pleased."

Myron hoped that Mr. Grinley would not be too glad to see them, but he feared the worst. Chances were very good that Mr. Grinley would bring up that Tea Cup business again. And this time he would give Myron, and probably Princess too, to the Air Force. The Air Force would send both of them to federal prison. Mr. Poindexter was right. They were taking the fall.

"I'll have some bad nights at first," Mr. Poindexter said, "but they'll pass."

"You're no more Humphrey Bogart then I am," Princess said.

"I have the trench coat. I have the hat. I have the gun." Those arguments seemed to satisfy Mr. Poindexter.

They arrived on the seventeenth floor and Mr. Poindexter herded Myron and Princess out of the elevator and down the hall to a wide wooden door with the words PETER PINCH, ATTORNEY AT LAW written on it. Mr. Poindexter had Myron open the door, and he pushed the two of them inside.

Two big guys with very short hair stood up when the three entered the waiting room. The suits couldn't hide the fact that the guys must have been weight lifters or wrestlers. One of them—the one who could talk,

Myron thought—said, "This is a private office. I will have to ask you to leave."

The waiting room was large and well furnished, obviously decorated to inspire confidence. The whole place was done in what his mother would have called American Colonial. Over the wooden chairs and the nicely upholstered couch were paintings of pilgrim types and tall men in powdered wigs. Myron heard voices coming from another room.

Mr. Poindexter began to explain what they were doing there, but was interrupted by Mr. Pinch, the other man who had been belaboring Uncle Hugo the day before. Mr. Pinch came into the waiting room and stopped when he saw Myron, Princess, and Mr. Poindexter. He glanced at the two muscle-bound guys and said, "Heel, Ivan." Ivan and his friend each took a step back, but they did not sit down.

Mr. Pinch said, "What are you three doing here?" He was not a happy man.

Delighted with himself, Mr. Poindexter said, "I trapped 'em."

"Oh?" said Mr. Pinch, unconvinced.

"Yeah," said Mr. Poindexter. "These kids are real interested in what Osgood does at night."

Mr. Pinch's eyes widened, and he called to Mr. Grinley. Mr. Grinley came into the room. Osgood stood behind him looking over his shoulder. Osgood seemed more worried than usual. Over one of his arms hung a

96

tasteful gray coat. A matching hat, clutched in his hand, vibrated weakly.

"Hi there, Osgood," said Myron. "How does it feel to be a traitor?"

"I'm sorry, Master Duberville. But I am doing what I feel is best for Astronetics. Your uncle Hugo really is quite mad, you know."

"He's not mad," Myron said. "He's just creative."

Mr. Grinley said, "There seems to be a difference of opinion about that. Hello, Princess. I am disappointed to see you here. We know that you were in the Tea Cup with Myron this afternoon. We were going to ignore that fact. Now you will have to share Myron's fate."

Princess said, "I never understood how you and my father could be brothers."

"Uncle Hugo isn't mad," Myron said again. "He just knows that the sound engineering lines of today tend to be the quaint curiosities of tomorrow."

"Is that so?" Mr. Grinley said.

"Yeah. Look at all those chances he took that turned out so well—the satellites, the jet airplanes, the transistors . . ."

Mr. Grinley chuckled unpleasantly and said, "He certainly does seem to have you well trained. But there is one thing that your Uncle Hugo has failed to point out to you. The things you mention did indeed turn out well. Those are advances in human technology. But never before has your uncle tried to make a deal with junk that he says are aliens from outer space. Do you see the difference?''

Myron could see the difference, though he didn't want to. Uncle Hugo sounded like a wacko again. He was stricken, and he was certain that he looked that way because both Mr. Grinley and Mr. Pinch nodded and smiled. Myron wished he could get Uncle Hugo into the same room with Mr. Grinley and Mr. Pinch so they could argue their cases in front of him. All this changing his mind made Myron feel like he was becoming a wacko too. "Yes," said Myron. "I see the difference."

"Well then, we're all friends again," said Mr. Grinley. "Put that gun away, Mr. Poindexter."

The detective smiled and pulled an unopened bag of peanuts from his pocket. No more bulge. He popped a peanut into his mouth and began to chomp.

Myron and Princess looked at each other and shook their heads.

Osgood put on his hat and ran out of the office without looking back.

Mr. Grinley had Mr. Pinch invite Myron and Princess into the private office. Mr. Poindexter waited in the waiting room with the two muscle men.

Mr. Pinch sat behind his enormous wooden desk with the brass fittings. Myron and Princess faced him from striped blue chairs. Mr. Grinley sat on the front of Mr.

Pinch's desk and allowed one leg to swing. From the next room, Myron could hear Mr. Poindexter's bag rattle when he pulled a fistful of peanuts from it.

Mr. Grinley said, "We know what a spellbinder Hugo Duberville can be, so we will give you one last chance before we turn you over to the Air Force."

"What's that?" said Myron.

"Just this. Mr. Pinch and I want you both at the stockholders' meeting so you can testify that Hugo Duberville is insane."

"You just want to run Astronetics yourself and make zillions of dollars," Princess said with some anger.

Evenly, Mr. Pinch said, "What we will do when we run Astronetics is none of your concern."

"My mother owns a lot of stock in Astronetics," Myron said. "Someday, I'll own it."

"I assure you, Myron," said Mr. Grinley, "that we will run Astronetics along sound engineering lines. We have no wish to kill a goose that lays golden eggs."

Myron did not like any of this. Not one bit. Though he now saw that Uncle Hugo really was a wacko, he was no longer convinced that this was a bad thing. Uncle Hugo, for all his craziness, was a nice person. Mr. Grinley and Mr. Pinch were not. Besides, Myron suspected that the amount of money Uncle Hugo spent on junk was a lot less than what Mr. Grinley and Mr. Pinch might spend on themselves if they got ahold of Astronetics.

Still, that was only a suspicion and might not be fair

to Mr. Grinley and Mr. Pinch. Maybe they, like Osgood, really wanted only what was best for the company. After all, even Myron thought that sending junk to other planets, especially aboard a nineteen sixty Chevrolet Belvedere, was more than a little strange. He said, "If I help you, you have to promise not to hurt Uncle Hugo."

"No problem," said Mr. Grinley.

"All right," Myron said. Princess nodded. They stood up. "I guess we'll be going now," Myron said.

"Of course. Poindexter?"

Mr. Poindexter kind of lounged in the doorway, blocking it entirely. There was a distracted smile on his face while he chewed his peanuts.

Myron thought that Mr. Grinley was going to ask Mr. Poindexter to take him and Princess home. Instead, Mr. Grinley said, "Poindexter, please take our two friends to Mr. Pinch's private apartment."

"What's going on?" Princess said with suspicion.

Mr. Grinley looked surprised that anyone would ask. "Well, as I said, I know what a spellbinder Hugo Duberville is. To make sure you two don't fall under his spell again before the stockholders' meeting, we're going to put you where he can't get at you."

Myron waited a beat. Then he grasped Princess by the hand and cried, "Let's go!" They ran toward the blocked door. Mr. Poindexter looked ready to stop them, but they each ducked around him on a different side. He didn't know which of them to grab first, and by the time he made up his mind, there was nothing to grab but air.

"Get them!" Mr. Grinley shouted.

Myron and Princess were halfway across the waiting room before Ivan and the other muscle man grabbed them. Ivan had Myron in a tight grip around his shoulder. Ivan's hand felt as if it were made of metal. Ivan's friend had Princess in a similar grip. Myron and Princess struggled, but they might as well have struggled against robots.

"We'll never help you!" Myron cried.

"You will," said Mr. Grinley, "or the Air Force will hear of your little Tea Cup escapade." To Ivan and his friend, Mr. Grinley said, "Take them away."

CHAPTER TEN
IN FOR THE DURATION

The two muscle men wrestled Myron and Princess along the hall back to the elevator. Myron tried to bite and kick, and he saw Princess doing the same, but he could tell these guys were professionals. Myron didn't connect very often, and when he did, Ivan and his friend didn't seem to feel a thing. Maybe they really *were* robots.

Soon Myron and Princess were in the elevator with Ivan and the other man, going up. According to the one button that was lit, they were going all the way to the top, to a floor called PENT. When the elevator stopped, the doors opend to reveal another set of doors. On the second set of doors was a sign that said, PENTHOUSE. NO ADMITTANCE. Ivan touched a blue handprint on one of the doors and they slid apart.

The muscle men pushed Myron and Princess into a short hallway. At one end of it was a metal emergency exit—boy do we need one of those, thought Myron—

and at the other was a regular wooden door, like the ones on the floors below.

Ivan unlocked the wooden door with a key, and said, "In here." The other man pushed Myron and Princess into what looked like a big hotel room. It was a fancy place with plenty of white furniture that had strangely carved legs, like the legs of mythical animals. Holding up the lamps were statues of boys dressed in turbans and flowing robes, like something out of the Arabian Nights. A thin, white ceramic wolfhound that was almost as tall as Myron stood next to a fireplace in which a rack of plaster logs lay ready for the following winter. Swag lamps and paintings on velvet of children with big sad eyes hung everywhere. In the corner was a fake bird enclosed in a cage made of threads on which dripped some terrible syrupy stuff.

"More money than taste," muttered Princess, as she looked around. Myron nodded.

Ivan's friend sat down on a chair in front of the door and folded his arms. Myron was surprised that the chair would hold him. The man had no particular expression on his face, but Myron had the feeling that getting past him would not be as easy as getting through a brick wall.

Ivan led Myron and Princess through the living room and showed them each an identical bedroom, both of which had more Arabian Nights lamps, more ceramic animals of varying sizes, more big-eyed children.

Mr. Pinch's private apartment reminded Myron of his

aunt Florence's house. Myron wasn't allowed to touch any of Aunt Florence's fragile knickknacks, or even to sit on the furniture in the living room. Whenever he was there, he felt that if he breathed wrong, Aunt Flo's whole place would somehow be thrown out of kilter. Mr. Pinch's place was the same.

Ivan was friendly enough in a cold professional way. He did not speak like a mug but like a trained radio announcer. Maybe there was intelligence behind all those muscles after all, Myron thought. But he didn't know if this was good or bad.

After showing them their bedroom, Ivan and his friend, Gert, paid little attention while Myron and Princess searched the apartment together.

They were on the thirty-fifth floor. Myron realized that even if the windows hadn't been the modern kind that don't open, there would be no place to go once you were outside. There was not even a ledge. And the air-conditioning vents were so small, a kid would have trouble getting his head through, let alone his entire body.

There were no windows at all in the bathroom. Big pink flamingos were painted on the wall and sandblasted into the glass around the stall shower. There were white guest towels, each with a pink *P* on it, little pink blobs of soap in the shape of rosebuds piled in an abalone shell, and a shaving kit.

The only way out was through the front door, and Gert, the brick wall, was sitting in front of that.

After their tour of the apartment, Myron and Princess sat despondently at the foot of the bed in Myron's room. The bedspread was white with pale purple dogs on it.

"Looks as if we're in for the duration," said Princess.

"Duration is right. It's almost two weeks till the stockholders' meeting. What do we do? Just sit here?"

"I vote we find Ivan and see what he knows."

Myron agreed. A few minutes later, they found Ivan sitting in the kitchen at the breakfast bar, drinking a cup of what seemed to be hot chocolate. Everything in the room gleamed. There was no place for the eye to rest. In its own way, the kitchen was just as uncomfortable as the rest of the apartment. Myron and Princess sat down on either side of Ivan.

"Hot Chocolatron?" Ivan said.

"That stuff's for kids," Princess said.

"I like it," said Ivan. "Better for you than coffee. No caffeine. Full of essential vitamins, minerals, and proteins. Doesn't taste bad, either."

There was a long silence during which Ivan sipped his Chocolatron. Myron looked at Princess. Princess looked at Myron.

Myron said, "You're going to keep us here for two weeks?"

Ivan nodded. "Uh-huh. Until the stockholders' meeting."

"We don't like it here," said Princess. "It's tacky."

"Tacky or not, this is where you stay."

"It's a prisoner's duty to try to escape," said Princess.

"We all have our duties," said Ivan. There was no emotion in his voice. He'd just as soon shoot them as drink Chocolatron.

"Do you think my uncle Hugo is crazy?" said Myron. If Ivan were not entirely sold on Mr. Grinley's point of view, maybe he could be talked into letting them go.

But Ivan said, "Mr. Grinley wouldn't want to put him away if he weren't."

"Makes sense," said Princess sarcastically.

"Put him away?" repeated Myron. "You mean like in some kind of hospital where they put crazy people?"

"An insane asylum?" asked Princess.

"Not necessarily," said Ivan. "Hospitals cost money. Sure you won't have some Chocolatron before bed?"

Myron and Princess both declined again and went back to Myron's bedroom. When they got in there, they closed the door. "What do you think?" Princess asked.

"I think that if hospitals cost money, then Uncle Hugo is dead meat."

"Uncle James wouldn't murder anybody."

"Maybe so. Maybe not. As you said before, 'Do you want to find out the hard way?'"

"Well, no."

"Then we have to get out of here and warn Uncle Hugo."

"If we leave, Uncle James will report us to the Air Force."

Myron shrugged. "I guess we all have our priorities."

Princess thought that over for a moment. Then she said, "All right, Houdini, I'm listening." When Princess heard Myron's plan, she stopped making fun of him and agreed to try it.

"What if they shoot us?" Princess said.

"In that case, we will have the satisfaction of getting blood all over their white carpet," Myron said.

Princess took a deep breath, opened the bedroom door, and whispered, "Here goes." Seconds later, Myron followed her.

When Myron walked through the living room, Princess was already in position near Gert. She was telling him her life story. Gert was watching her carefully as she paraded up and down in front of him, regaling him with tales of family outings, minor injuries, and indignities suffered at the hands of brothers and sisters.

Gert was not really interested in what she was saying. He reminded Myron of a frog watching a fly that had buzzed too close for its own good. Ivan was sitting on a white couch in the living room, thumbing through *People* magazine. He nodded at Myron when Myron walked through the living room heading for the bathroom.

The bathroom was close to the front door, next to the kitchen. Myron went inside, closed the door, switched on the light, and turned on the fan that sucked bad-smelling air out. The fan hummed loudly.

Myron opened the shaving kit and took out the electric shaver. It was the kind that could run either on batteries or on wall current. Myron set it for AC because alternating current was the kind that came out of the wall. He turned on the switch, and the shaver began to whine like a big bumblebee. It did not sound very loud against the humming of the fan.

He looked at the shaver for a few seconds, then opened the toilet and looked down at the blue water inside. If what he had in mind didn't work, Myron would have a lot of explaining to do. Mr. Grinley might not wait for the stockholders' meeting or even for the Air Force trial. He might just do to Myron what he had in mind for Uncle Hugo.

Better not to think about it. Myron dropped the whining electric shaver into the toilet. Instantly, sparks leaped from the socket where it was plugged in, the shaver stopped whining, the fan stopped humming, and the room went black.

Muffled shouting came from outside the bathroom. Ivan's shouting continued as Myron quickly opened the door and ran toward the front door. Two quick gunshots punctuated the confusion. One of the bullets thumped into the wall near him. The front door was open when he got there, so Princess had probably already gotten away. He ran down the short hallway toward where the EXIT sign glowed like the red ghost of an EXIT sign.

Myron pushed through the weighted emergency door under the EXIT sign and began to run down the wide metal steps. The stairwell looked as if it were radioactive, lit as it was by blue emergency lamps screwed at intervals into the cinderblock walls. The light cast eerie shadows, but he had no time to enjoy the atmosphere.

As he ran, he noticed that the paint on the railings and rungs of the steps was hardly worn at all. Evidently, people did not come down this way very often. Myron stopped for a second and heard someone below him descending the stairs very quickly. Heavy footsteps echoed above him.

He glanced down over the railing and saw a hand—looking like death in the strange blue light—and Princess's denim jacket about a floor below him. Myron called out, "Princess! Wait!"

He leaped down after her. "Hurry," she cried unnecessarily. Above, they could hear Ivan and Gert coming after them.

Myron and Princess leaped two or three stairs at a time down flight after flight. He was not in any shape to keep this up for long, and he suspected that Princess (whom he had once thought of as a real porker) was not either. But the booming of Ivan and Gert behind them kept him moving pretty quickly. Myron stopped thinking about what he was doing and just did it.

Once, somebody fired at them. The bullet ricocheted off the metal railing and the sound echoed for a long time.

Myron and Princess came to a door that had the

word LOBBY stenciled on it. They gasped for breath. They'd run down thirty-five floors!

Ivan and Gert were no more than a floor or two above them. Princess pushed the door open and began to go through the doorway, but Myron panted, "That's too obvious. Maybe we can lose ourselves in the basement."

"Right," Princess said. They continued to race downward. They stopped around the first turn, under the landing where the lobby door was, flattened themselves against the wall, and waited while they tried to catch their breath.

Myron heard Ivan and Gert stop when they arrived at the lobby door. He heard the door open and then hiss as it closed on its door closer. For a few seconds, Myron heard nothing. Princess nodded. "Well," she said, "that was—"

Suddenly, Ivan and Gert were galloping down the stairs, firing their pistols.

"Come on," Myron cried as he dragged Princess after him. Princess did not need to be dragged. Soon, they had put a little distance between themselves and their pursuers. The stairs were dirty here, as if workers had come this way. They passed SUBBASEMENT ONE. At SUBBASEMENT TWO, Myron saw that the stairway continued downward. He pushed the door open and it made a terrible groaning sound. He and Princess rushed through quickly, and the door sighed as they pushed it closed.

They breathed hard while they waited for Ivan and Gert. Seconds later, Ivan and Gert clumped down the stairs, sounding like a herd of galloping horses. The sound got fainter and soon was gone.

"Another trick?" Princess said.

"We were lucky once because they were making so much noise," Myron said. "Do you really want to chance making that door groan again?"

Princess shook her head. She and Myron looked around.

CHAPTER ELEVEN
HER!

They were at the end of a long, low corridor lit by regular fluorescent tubes. Evidently the electrical havoc Myron had caused by shorting out the shaver had not reached this deep into the building. Pipes and cables ran down the walls and ceiling trailing great shadows across the floor. Hydrants and valves stuck out from the walls like the trophy heads of dead animals. An electrical buzz hung in the heavy warm air.

Myron said, "This place looks like a zoo for Uncle Hugo's aliens." He smiled, remembering Uncle Hugo.

Though Princess laughed a little at what Myron had said, it was not a happy laugh. She said, "When Ivan and Gert get to the bottom and don't find us, they'll probably come back and try the subbasements. I, for one, would rather take my chances with the aliens." Princess began to walk along the corridor.

"Right," said Myron. He followed her. They saw control boards with flashing lights, and chittering metal boxes with metal-bound cables snaking out of them. Myron could not see the end of the corridor. The walls seemed to meet at a dark point off in the distance.

"Say, look at this." Princess had stopped before the biggest pair of elevator doors Myron had ever seen. They did not open sideways the way regular elevator doors did, but up and down, like a mouth. Next to the elevator were the usual two control buttons. Princess and Myron looked at the door for a moment.

"The jaws of death," Myron said morosely. He pushed the UP button. To his surprise, the UP button lit up, and immediately a mechanical noise began in the shaft.

"Well," Princess said.

They waited for the elevator without saying anything more. Myron wanted to ask Princess what she thought they would find when they got out of the elevator, if getting out was possible. But he knew she was as ignorant as he was. Asking would just be silly.

The elevator arrived and the jaws of death opened. The car was big enough to carry a small automobile, but it was not fancy. It had a wooden floor and pads on the walls. Myron and Princess did not wait to be invited inside. "Don't push ONE," said Myron, "push LOBBY."

"I know," said Princess irritably.

As the elevator carried them upward, Myron, against his better judgment, began to feel pretty good. After all, he and Princess had uncovered a plot against his uncle Hugo, and they had escaped two armed and muscular men. Still, he did not let his good feelings dance around; he knew that he and Princess were not safe yet. They might not even be safe in Uncle Hugo's house. They might never be safe.

The elevator ground to a stop and the big door yawned to reveal an empty corridor with chipped yellow walls. The words SAFETY FIRST were stenciled in a few places. It was very quiet. Far away, Myron could hear traffic. The air-conditioning sounded like a hurricane.

They tiptoed down the hallway. The elevator door closed, and they jumped at the noise, then smiled at each other and continued. Around two corners was the lobby. It was high and wide. Banks of brushed-chrome elevators lined the gray marbled walls.

At the front of the lobby, a uniformed guard was sitting behind a fancy desk that had TV screens built into it. He was eating a sandwich. It smelled like corned beef, heavy on the mustard. Myron wished he had not turned down the Chocolatron. The important part about the guard was that he had his back to Myron and Princess.

At the back of the lobby was a glass door that had a push bar across its middle. Outside the door was an ornamental garden with pineapple-shaped palm trees and flowers around the edges. Colored lights shone on the fronds and leaves and blossoms, making alien-shaped shadows on the wall of the Magnificent Raff Building. At the other side of the garden was what looked like a barred gate.

Myron was surprised that it was still dark outside. He looked at his watch: 10:37. So much had happened since he and Princess had started their adventure that evening, it seemed that entire days had gone by.

Across the top of the glass door an engraved notice said FIRE EXIT ONLY. Myron put his mouth up close to Princess's ear and said, "We'll have to chance it." Princess nodded.

Myron led the way to the door. Princess was right behind him. The guard kept eating his sandwich. A magazine page cracked as he turned it. Myron gripped the push bar in both hands, closed his eyes, and pushed it. Immediately, a loud alarm bell rang. Myron and Princess ran across the square gray stones toward the iron gate. Behind them, the guard stood in the doorway for a moment, blowing his whistle. He ran after them.

Myron pushed down on a wrought-iron handle and shoved hard against the resisting gate. As he and Princess ran off, the guard called after them, "I better not catch you kids playing around here again!"

They were in a driveway with the Magificent Raff Building rising thirty-five stories on one side and the back of a Chinese restaurant on the other. The smells coming from the restaurant were delicious. Myron and Princess ran to a street that crossed one end of the driveway.

They barreled around the corner onto a broad boulevard. The name of the Chinese restaurant, O Fat, was written in red neon letters in fake Chinese style across the front of the building.

Myron and Princess looked both ways. Coming around the corner, rubbernecking like tourists, were Ivan and Gert. Each had one hand in a pocket.

"I don't think those guys are carrying bags of peanuts," Myron said.

"Absolutely," Princess said.

They turned and ran toward the crowd of fancy people waiting for their cars in front of O Fat.

When Ivan and Gert saw Myron and Princess, they began to run too.

Suddenly, someone leaped out at them from the shadow of a fancifully carved and painted statue of a dragon crawling down O Fat's wall.

Myron jumped and cried, "That's her! The wacko woman!" Princess didn't jump, but she stared at the old woman wide-eyed, as if she could not believe her bad luck. Ivan and Gert were getting closer.

"You kids keep running," the woman said, and stepped toward Ivan and Gert as she pulled a big rubber package from one of her coat pockets.

Myron and Princess ran a short way, then stopped and looked over their shoulders. The old woman tossed the rubber package into the path of the men. In seconds, it blew up into a rubber life raft. This did not even slow down Ivan and Gert. They just jumped over it as if they were Olympic champions.

Myron and Princess began to run again. By this time, they were running among the fancy people in front of O Fat. People shrieked. One man hollered, "Watch it, kids!" as Myron and Princess rushed by him.

On the other side of the crowd, Myron looked back. He saw the black woman running after them. She flung a tangle of wire in the path of the men. The wire tripped them and they fell headlong into the crowd.

"Keep moving," the old woman said as she pushed Myron and Princess along. She herded them up against the wall of O Fat, said "Quickly, behind me," then turned to face Ivan and Gert.

Myron and Princess huddled behind the woman as she faced Ivan and Gert proudly, chin upraised. She pulled a wrench from another pocket and with it reached into the mouth of one of O Fat's plaster dragons, as if she were some kind of dragon dentist.

Suddenly, water gushed from the dragon's mouth and hit the two men hard, forcing them back into the fancy restaurant crowd. There was a lot more shrieking as everybody slipped around on the wet sidewalk. Some people fell over. Ivan and Gert could not get away from the crowd because a women wearing a long black dress was using them to pull herself back to her feet. Her spiky-heeled shoes didn't help any of them.

"You'd better scram," the old woman said. "Go to the Unidentified Flying Omelet. I'll be along as soon as I can."

"But—" said Myron.

"Go!" the woman shouted. Princess dragged Myron away. "Scramming sounds like a good idea," she said, "no matter where we go."

As they ran, the old woman marched back into the crowd crying, "What's going on? What's going on?"

Myron and Princess ran to the corner. Cipher City was pretty well lit at night, which was one of the reasons normal people went there. This corner was no exception. Myron and Princess crouched behind a low wall that held up the elevated front lawn of the Magnificent Raff Building.

"Now what?" Myron said.

"We're free," Princess said. "We ought to go back to your house to warn Uncle Hugo." She did not sound enthusiastic about this option.

"Yeah," Myron said. He peeked over the wall. The old woman was talking to Ivan and Gert and a couple of big Oriental gentlemen who were dressed in tuxedos. She was screaming in a high-pitched voice and waving her arms in the air. "My momma told me there'd be nights like this!"

118

"Or," Princess went on, "we could go to the Unidentified Flying Omelet and call your uncle Hugo from a pay phone."

"Yeah," Myron said. He crouched behind the wall again. "I've never even heard of the place."

"I never have either, but it can't be far. That woman knows we're on foot."

Myron thought for a minute. On the one hand, Uncle Hugo needed to be warned. Now. Tonight. If Mr. Grinley couldn't find him and Princess, he might do something drastic. Besides, the woman was obviously a bigger wacko than his uncle. Myron said, "Yeah. It's not far, but who knows what kind of place the Unidentified Flying Omelet is?"

"Sure," said Princess. "Maybe there's an opium den in the back. Maybe the old woman wants to shanghai us into the crew of a tramp steamer. Maybe," Princess added pointedly, "she's an alien."

Together, they shook their heads and said, "Nah."

That was on the one hand. On the other hand, it was about time Myron found out exactly who that woman was and what she wanted. She might be helpful if only because she could drive him and Princess back to Uncle Hugo's house. And there was probably a telephone at the Unidentified Flying Omelet. Calling Uncle Hugo would be even faster than driving across town. Myron said, "I promised you an adventure, didn't I?"

Princess nodded and said, "This is exciting all right,

but that woman doesn't look like the kind of person who would own a hand that glowed in the dark."

That clinched it. "Well she is," Myron said. "Let's go find that place before Ivan and Gert get tired of explaining themselves to those two Chinese waiters."

"What about your uncle Hugo?"

"We can call him from the Unidentified Flying Omelet and then find out who that woman is."

"Kill two birds with one stone," Princess said.

"Not a happy metaphor," Myron said.

Myron and Princess walked quickly for a few blocks to put a little distance between them and their pursuers, then stopped to study a big laminated map on the corner of Nada and Bupkis. There was a big laminated map on every corner in Cipher City. Princess checked the listing under restaurants while Myron studied the map.

"It's not here," Princess said.

"It's probably not the kind of place that *would* be here," Myron said glumly. Princess pointed up the street. "There are a lot of funny little shops and stuff just outside Cipher City, up on Marsupial Boulevard."

"Sounds like a good bet," Myron said.

They looked around, hoping they wouldn't see Ivan and Gert, then walked toward Marsupial Boulevard along the wide, bone-white sidewalks of Cipher City.

Tall office buildings surrounded them. A few windows in each building were lit, which only made the place seem lonelier. Far off, they could hear the muffled rumble of traffic. Every so often, Myron or Princess would look over a shoulder to see if anyone was following them. Nobody was. Cipher City seemed to be deserted.

At last, Princess said, "Imagine, that old woman using junk to stop those two punks."

"Well, some of it worked."

"Yeah. Do you think it's just a coincidence that we're suddenly involved with so many people who are interested in junk?"

"She seemed interested in Uncle Hugo, too," Myron said.

"Then it's not just a coincidence," Princess said. "It's part of the Ethical Structure of the Universe."

Myron looked at Princess. "What's that?"

"That," said Princess with a perfectly straight face, "is what I call the collection of secret rules by which the universe works. Not just rules of physics and chemistry, but of morality and ethics too."

Myron blinked at Princess twice. She looked so serious that he didn't know what to make of her explanation. Then Princess began to laugh. This made Myron laugh. He nearly gagged when he tried to say, "The Ethical Structure of the Universe." This only made both of them laugh harder. Soon, they were both laughing like fools.

After they had walked off their laughter, they were quiet for a long time. Myron said, "Maybe the old woman really is an alien. After all, I saw her hand glow in the dark."

"You know, of course," said Princess, "that I'm going to ask her about that when we're all together at the Unidentified Flying Omelet."

"I don't care. It's true."

Soon they were standing on Marsupial Boulevard, on the edge of Cipher City, looking out at the strange stores and shops across the street. Across the street was like a different world. Big, sharp-branched trees reached for the sky among tall, old-fashioned street lamps, each of which made an island of light every few buildings, but left most of the block in darkness.

Princess pulled her jacket more tightly around her. "Is it just my imagination, or is it colder out here than it is inside Cipher City?"

"I don't know, but I feel it too. Where's the Unidentified Flying Omelet?"

They looked up and down the block across the street. Myron said, "Maybe that's it," and pointed to a green neon sign.

"It looks like the only place that's open, that's for sure."

They crossed Marsupial Boulevard easily—there wasn't much traffic at eleven o'clock at night—and walked along the sidewalk across the street. They passed used-hardware stores and a place that sold Latvian antiques. Many stores were just dark holes with windows full of dust and dead flies. The sidewalk was broken and raised up in places by the roots of the trees. Leaves rattled in the wind. Outside the islands of light, it was easy to imagine that Ivan and Gert, or worse things, were all around them, hunkering down in the darkness, waiting to pounce.

At last Myron and Princess came to a big round building that looked as if it were made of two pie tins stuck together edge to edge. Its round windows were all steamed up. Over the door three bits of green neon showed a flying saucer taking off. In one bit, the neon tube formed a picture of the saucer on the ground. In the next, the saucer was a little way into the air. In the third, it was above the white neon cloud. Inside the cloud were the yellow neon words UNIDENTIFIED FLYING OMELET.

"This place is familiar," Princess said.

"Yeah," said Myron. "It looks just like the Tea Cup."

"Another coincidence?" said Princess.

"I'm betting on the Ethical Structure of the Universe," said Myron.

CHAPTER TWELVE
THE ETHICAL STRUCTURE
OF THE UNIVERSE

Inside, the Unidentified Flying Omelet was warm and it smelled like the best breakfast ever. The place was crowded with the kind of people Myron had seen on his bus ride. But instead of looking sullen and angry, they were all laughing and talking and eating. They didn't seem threatening at all. Some of them were sitting at the counter around a pit in the center of the room where all the cooking was going on. Others sat in booths up against the outside wall.

But Myron decided the best thing about the Un-identified Flying Omelet were the waitresses. Each one wore a gray blouse and gray shorts. Their legs were covered in gray sparkling tights. Each one wore a Robin Hood hat with a little metal feather sticking out of it. The waitresses were on roller skates, and whenever they moved, they made a noise like thunder.

Even though it was the middle of the night, Myron

and Princess agreed that a big breakfast sounded pretty good. They had to shout to be heard above the noise of people talking and laughing and silverware knocking together and waitresses rolling around.

While Princess went to get a table, Myron found a pay telephone back near the bathrooms. One bathroom was called Gleeps and the other was called Glerps, but the pictures on the door made it pretty clear which was which.

Myron called his uncle. He waited through ten rings; nobody answered. It was a little late for a junk hunt, but you never knew with Uncle Hugo. Maybe he was out looking for old light bulbs or flashlights or something. Then it occurred to Myron that Uncle Hugo—and maybe Princess's father—might be out looking for *them.* It was very late.

Myron found Princess in a booth at the edge of the room and sat down across from her. In the center of the table was a big silver bowl full of popcorn.

"Well?" Princess said.

"Nobody home. I don't understand it. Unless Uncle Hugo and your father are looking for us."

"My mom and dad are out for the evening. I should probably call them and leave a message telling them where we are. Maybe Dad can get ahold of your uncle Hugo. Doesn't he have an answering machine?"

"I guess not. Odd, huh? We'll just have to warn him in person."

"If that's the case," Princess said, "why are we wasting our time here?"

"Gathering useful information. Besides, walking or busing back to Uncle Hugo's house would take hours."

"What else can we do?"

"Maybe the woman will give us a ride."

"I wouldn't go anywhere with her without the testimony of a character witness or a police escort."

Myron thought that over. He said, "We could call the police."

"Nobody's done anything illegal yet."

"We were kidnapped."

"Prove it. If you were a policeman, who would you believe? Two kids with a wild story or a couple of guys wearing ties?"

"I guess," said Myron mournfully.

"I hope this old woman is worth waiting around for." Princess got up and roamed back to where the telephones were. While she was gone, Myron munched on the popcorn in the silver bowl. It was hot and fresh. The food was working out, even if nothing else was.

A few minutes later, Princess returned. She said, "Well, that's all we can do till we get home." She picked up a handful of popcorn and stuffed it into her mouth. "That crazy woman knows her restaurants, anyway. There's real butter on this popcorn," she said.

A waitress rolled over to their table and stopped with a swivel of her hips. The name ESTELLE was stitched to her pocket. She lifted her order book and cried, "Two coffees?"

Myron knew that waitresses and waiters often said this to adults, but no one had ever said it to him before. From the surprised look on her face, Myron knew that no one had ever said it to Princess either. They shrugged. Myron said, "Sure."

"Make mine black," said Princess.

Estelle dropped two menus and rolled away.

"Black?" said Myron.

"We've struck the main nerve here," said Princess. "No point going halfway."

The menus were interesting too. You could get a steak or a fried zucchini or a hot dog or almost anything else. But everything came wrapped in a scrambled egg.

Estelle came back with two cups of coffee. They were both black. Cream and sugar were on the table in silver pots. Princess ordered the poached avocado flambé omelet and Myron ordered the taco surprise omelet. Estelle nodded and rolled away without saying a word.

Princess sipped her coffee and made a face. "I don't understand why adults drink this stuff."

Myron tasted his coffee. It was hot and bitter but he kept sipping it. If Princess was going to experience the main nerve, he himself could do no less.

The food came. The surprising part of Myron's taco surprise omelet was that it had chocolate sprinkles all over the top instead of cheese. Princess's poached avocado flambé omelet was on fire when it arrived. "How do I eat this?" Princess said, studying it warily.

"Give it a chance," Estelle said. "Just don't blow on it and burn down the restaurant." She rolled away.

It wasn't long before the fire went out. Cautiously, each of them dug into the food. "This is terrific!" Myron said. "Who'd have thought that tacos with chocolate sprinkles would be any good?"

"Not me," said Princess. "I still don't believe it. But this poached avocado is great." Then Myron had a little of Princess's omelet and Princess had a little of Myron's.

After that, they both got very involved in eating. When Myron stopped to have another sip of coffee, he looked up. The old woman was standing at their table, smiling at them. Her ancient coat was open to show the same flower-print dress that Myron had seen her wearing on the way home from the airport. She said, "I'm glad to see that you weren't shy about ordering. Clarence Terence O'melet likes hearty eaters."

Suddenly embarrassed, Myron put down his fork. "Uh, won't you join us?" he asked.

"Why?" said the old woman. "Are you coming apart?" She laughed and shook her head, then shooed Myron to the end of the booth so that she could sit down next to him.

"This is a really wonderful place," Princess said.

"Glad you like it. It is run by my friend, Clarence Terence O'melet."

"Is that his real name?" Myron said.

"No. His real name is Clarence Terence Unidentified.

128

You see, he is an orphan, and no one knew his parents. But he thought that the name O'melet would be better for business."

Myron nodded. Wacko. Pure one-hundred-percent all-beef wacko. He couldn't wait for Princess to ask about the glowing hand.

The woman took a handful of popcorn and began to lick the pops into her mouth one at a time. Between pops, she said, "I am Letitia Reticuli."

Myron wondered briefly if he should give his real name, then decided that there was no reason not to. "I am Myron Duberville."

"And I am Princess Grinley. What exactly is your interest in Myron's uncle Hugo?"

Just then Estelle rolled back to the table. She and Letitia Reticuli seemed to know each other. Ms. Reticuli didn't even look at the menu before she ordered the open-faced pizza omelet. Estelle rolled away.

"Ah, yes. Myron's uncle Hugo," the mystery woman said, and nodded as if she were agreeing with Princess. "Let's just say that I have an interest in junk."

"Actually," said Princess as she resumed eating, "I was kind of curious about that. Myron says he saw you on his way in from the airport with his uncle Hugo. Then he saw you again in Uncle Hugo's backyard. Now, here you show up again when we need rescuing. Co-incidence?"

Ms. Reticuli stopped eating popcorn and said,

"Never. It is part of the Ethical Structure of the Universe."

"I thought I made that up," Princess said, surprised.

"Most assuredly not, child. Everything is part of the Ethical Structure of the Universe, all whirling around each other and trying to stay in balance. But that is not how I happened to be around when you needed me. I was told you were in trouble by the equipment in the service corridor beneath the Magnificent Raff Building."

"I told you they were aliens," Myron said to Princess.

"Good," Ms. Reticuli said. "You know about the aliens. But the truth is, I could have tracked you even without the equipment in the service corridor."

"Oh?" Myron and Princess said together.

"Yes. Myron is carrying an alien in his pocket."

While Myron pulled things from his pockets as if they were on fire, Letitia Reticuli explained that since Myron had picked it up, the alien had been absorbing his brain waves, amplifying them, and using them to broadcast his location. She inspected the pocket comb, money, keys, and bits of paper that Myron laid out on the table. "I don't see it," she said.

"Maybe it's not here," Princess said.

"Oh, it's here, all right. I can feel its presence. It's *that* kind of alien."

Myron felt a rising excitement as he realized that he knew what the alien was. He opened his wallet and found the whatsit he'd gotten from the elevator repairman.

"That's it," Ms. Reticuli said with joy as she took the whatsit from Myron and studied it. "How are you doing?" she said to it. A moment later, she nodded and put the whatsit into her pocket. Myron thought to protest but decided not to. However, he did say, "Mighty lucky I picked that up."

"Not luck," Ms. Reticuli said. "The Ethical Structure of the Universe, plus the peculiar talents of this little guy." She patted the pocket in which she held the whatsit. "Now," she said, "tell me what you know of aliens."

Before Myron could answer, Estelle came back with a pizza built on a scrambled egg instead of on a crust. A man was following her. He was dressed in a gray suit, as if he worked for Astronetics, but the suit had grease spots all over it. He had a big friendly face with little round glasses over his eyes. He parted his hair exactly in the middle of his head, and it curled up at each side like the tips of a mustache.

Letitia Reticuli leaped from her seat with a whoop and gave the man a big hug. Before she sat down, she said, "Children, this is Clarence Terence O'melet, the owner of the Unidentified Flying Omelet." She introduced them to him.

Clarence Terence O'melet bowed to Myron and kissed Princess's hand. He said, "I am delighted to meet both of you. But you in particular, Myron. Your uncle Hugo is the one who got me and the Air Force together."

"Oh?" said Myron.

"Yes. You've probably never heard about it because it's top secret, but I am the designer of the biggest project at Astronetics, the Tea Cup."

Myron and Princess glanced at each other, eyes wide with amazement. Myron settled into his seat and said, "I thought you owned the Unidentified Flying Omelet."

"I do. This restaurant is my life. But I dabble in aeronautical engineering as a hobby. That's why this place is the shape it is."

"You and Ms. Reticuli are old friends, hm?" said Princess.

"Why yes. She eats here all the time."

"As a matter of fact," Letitia Reticuli said, "we were just discussing Myron's uncle Hugo when you walked up."

"He's a visionary," Clarence Terence O'melet said. He looked around and smiled. "Well, I have other customers to attend to. Please come in again, all of you. And do bring Mr. Duberville. I haven't seen him since we finished negotiations on the Tea Cup."

When Clarence Terence O'melet was gone, Myron said, "I guess that the Tea Cup is not quite as secret as Mr. Grinley thinks it is."

"There is a character reference for you," said Ms. Reticuli, jabbing the air after Clarence Terence O'melet with her fork. "Plus the fact that I have saved you from the men who were chasing you. Plus the fact that you know that I know that your uncle Hugo is collecting junk. Plus the fact that I know that when you see equipment you think aliens. This is not normal or usual. I suspect that your uncle Hugo and I have similar interests. If I am wrong, you and I can go our separate ways. Now, will you please tell me what you know of aliens? Then, perhaps, I can tell you about myself."

"I have just one easy question I would like you to answer first," said Princess. "Just so I know where I stand."

Myron and Letitia Reticuli looked at Princess, waiting. Here it comes, thought Myron.

Princess said, "Does your hand glow in the dark?"

"It can if I want it to."

"Could you do it for us now?"

"It's not the kind of thing one does in public."

"I suppose not. Tell her anything you want, Myron. She must be the only one in town who doesn't know what's going on at Astronetics."

Myron decided Princess was right. "All right," he said. He told Ms. Reticuli about how there was this big power struggle inside Astronetics, with Mr. Grinley and his "sound engineering principles" on one side, and Uncle Hugo and his free-floating creativity on the other. (The "sound engineering principles" of today are the quaint curiosities of tomorrow.) Myron and Princess had followed Uncle Hugo's butler, Osgood, had been captured by Mr. Grinley and his friend Mr. Pinch, and had come to suspect that Mr. Grinley planned to murder Uncle Hugo.

"Those were Mr. Grinley's hired goons you saved us from," Myron said.

Ms. Reticuli nodded. Her mouth was busy pulling in yards and yards of stringy mozzarella cheese.

Myron went on to explain Uncle Hugo's ideas about how aliens had come to Earth and how they were ignored because they looked like junk and oddball hardware. "He wants to send them home in exchange for spaceships full of titanium."

Letitia Reticuli stopped with the fork halfway to her lips, a look of shock and surprise on her face. She bit off the mozzarella string, swallowed mightily, and said, "He has a way to send them home?"

"Yes," said Myron. "Aboard a modified white nineteen sixty Chevrolet Belvedere."

She nodded and put down her fork. "It is exactly as I had hoped. Those lost puppies are going home at last."

CHAPTER THIRTEEN
THE CAPTAIN

"You mean," said Princess, "you know about this stuff?"

"I've been searching for years for a person like Myron's uncle Hugo."

"You have?" Myron said.

"I have. But I had to make sure that I had found him before I revealed myself."

"Revealed yourself?" Myron said.

"Revealed what?" Princess said. Myron knew that she was thinking about the woman's glowing hand. That's certainly what Myron was thinking about.

"Come with me now to my quarters over the Unidentified Flying Omelet, where my revelations will be less public. I will show you things that will satisfy even you kids."

Myron said, "If you'll excuse us for just a moment, I think Princess and I should talk this over."

As she slid over to let Myron out of the booth, Ms. Reticuli said, "Be quick, children. The Ethical Structure of the Universe is powerful, but time is short."

Myron and Princess walked back to where the telephone was and put their heads together. "What do you think?" Myron said.

"This woman is just as crazy as your uncle Hugo, but I also think we owe it to ourselves to find out what she has to reveal. Besides, I want to see her hand glow in the dark." Princess chuckled.

Myron didn't like the sound of that chuckle, but he really couldn't blame Princess. He said, "You really trust her enough to go to her apartment? And if we don't trust her that far, how can we trust her to drive us home?"

"I don't trust her any farther than spit."

"Then we have a problem, don't we?" Myron said. He saw Clarence Terence O'melet coming toward them. "But maybe there's a solution." He beckoned to Clarence Terence O'melet.

Clarence Terence O'melet smiled and said, "Good evening, young lady and gentleman. I hope that your omelets were satisfactory."

"They were great," Myron said. "But we do have a question for you."

"I'm sorry," Clarence Terence O'melet said as he folded his arms and closed his eyes. "My secret spices must remain a secret. But perhaps you would care to hear about the Tea Cup?"

"Some other time," said Myron. "But we would like to hear about Letitia Reticuli."

"A fine woman," Clarence Terence O'melet said. "A great appreciator of omelets."

"But can we trust her with our lives?" Princess asked.

"I have trusted her with *my* life, if that's any help to you. Why do you ask?"

"We like to know who we're running off with," Princess said.

"I have never run off with Letitia, but I am sure that you will be entirely safe with her. Anything else?"

"No, thanks," said Myron.

After Clarence Terence O'melet had walked away, Princess said, "I'm not sure I trust *him* any farther than spit either."

"He says he's worked with Uncle Hugo. I think he's okay."

"I guess it's a calculated risk."

"I wouldn't push the word 'calculated' too far." Myron looked toward the front door. "Besides, Ivan and Gert could walk in here any time. They don't strike me as the type that gives up easy."

Princess nodded, then smiled and nudged Myron with her elbow. She said, "Yeah. And I still want to see that old woman's hand glow."

"I know," said Myron as they walked back to the table. Ms. Reticuli was just finishing her open-faced pizza omelet. She looked up at them and smiled. "Well, I hope you're coming with me. Oh, this is a great day."

"We're coming."

"I am delighted." She touched her lips with a paper napkin, then bustled to the pit at the center of the restaurant where all the cooking was going on. She deftly avoided the quickly moving omelet chefs, and came to the center of the pit, where there was a ladder that she began to climb. As she rose through the steam and out of sight through a hole in the ceiling, Estelle brought the check.

Myron and Princess looked at each other and shook their heads. They pooled their dwindling cash reserves to pay the bill and leave Estelle a nice tip.

"Letitia Reticuli owes us three dollars and fifty-eight cents," Princess said.

"I hope her revelation is worth that much."

Feeling as if everyone were watching them, Myron and Princess crossed to the kitchen and stood at the bottom of the ladder with the chefs running every which way around them.

"Ladies first?" Princess asked as if she were hoping this would not be the case.

"Naw," said Myron, feeling noble and stupid at the same time. "I'll go." He took a rung in his hands and began to climb. The ladder shook as Princess climbed behind him.

Myron poked his head through the hole in the ceiling,

and he was in darkness. He heard Ms. Reticuli (he hoped it was she) moving around and swearing as she ran into things.

"What's the matter?" Princess called from below.

"Hang on. I can't see."

"What?"

Myron heard a light switch being flicked. Suddenly the room was filled with weak yellow light coming from old-fashioned fixtures in the walls, making the place look as if it were under water. The room seemed to cover the entire top floor of the building. The sound of roller skates and laughter was coming in through the fringed curtains in front of the front windows.

Princess followed Myron up through the hole. Myron liked Ms. Reticuli's apartment. It was comfy, containing as it did lots of big overstuffed chairs and couches covered with bold patterns of flowers. But there was no place to sit because the furniture, which by itself filled the round room, was covered with junk, just like the furniture in Uncle Hugo's library.

Ms. Reticuli moved a broken toaster and a length of garden hose onto the floor and invited Myron and Princess to sit down on a long couch that had feet like the claws of an animal gripping wooden balls. She hung her coat over the glass globe of a gum-ball machine that was standing next to the couch.

"Can I get you children anything?"

"No, thanks," Princess said. "But now that we're not

in public anymore, I, for one, would like to see your hand glow."

Ms. Reticuli sat down in an enormous chair and nearly sank out of sight. She said, "Give me a minute to rest, child. I'm not as young as I was."

"Well then," said Princess, "maybe while we're waiting, you can tell us more about how the alien in Myron's pocket led you to us."

"The signal was very clear," said Ms. Reticuli.

"Maybe you were able to find us," Myron said, "but that doesn't explain exactly why you took the trouble. Or exactly why you collect junk."

"I collect junk for the same reason your uncle Hugo collects it. Because most of it is not really junk, but aliens. I want to send them home."

"I never would have guessed that anybody but my uncle Hugo would have that kind of interest."

"Oh, a lot of people collect junk as a hobby. That's why, before I made contact, I wanted to make sure that your uncle was not just one of those. The fact that he had a modified nineteen sixty Chevrolet Belvedere clinched it for me. He and I must work together."

Myron and Princess were nodding. This was actually beginning to sound rational to Myron. Suddenly he cried out, "There it is!"

"There what is?" Princess said.

Myron got up and ran over to a multiheaded water main. It gleamed even in the watery light of Ms. Reticuli's apartment. He touched the cold brown metal gently. "This is it. It's the captain. I'm sure of it!"

"What captain?" said Princess.

"To pilot the modified nineteen sixty Chevrolet Belvedere. It's the only thing Uncle Hugo needs before he can send the aliens home."

Deep in her chair, Ms. Reticuli nodded. She said, "I thought that might be what was holding up your uncle Hugo's parade. But you're wrong, Myron. That isn't the captain. It is the first officer, a creature named Schyler."

"How do you know?" Myron asked.

"I know," said Letitia Reticuli, "because *I* am the captain."

CHAPTER FOURTEEN
PRINCESS TELLS ALL

"You must be kidding," said Princess.

"Of course she's kidding," said Myron. "All aliens look like junk."

Letitia Reticuli shook her head and said, "That makes as much sense as saying that all aliens look like Mr. Spock."

For a while, nobody said anything. Myron listened to the roller-skate thunder and laughter coming in through the front window. Roller skates he could understand. It made sense. It made him feel good.

This other stuff was just crazy. And Ms. Reticuli was being so slippery about showing off her glowing hand that Myron was beginning to doubt that he had ever really seen it. The only thing that he couldn't figure out was the fact that Ms. Reticuli not only was a wacko, but she believed the same wacko stuff as his uncle Hugo.

Coincidence? Ethical Structure of the Universe? Whatever. It was too many for him.

"Uh," said Princess, "do you have a telephone I can use?" She looked at Myron and winked.

"Of course, child," Ms. Reticuli said. "On the little table outside the bathroom."

Princess stepped carefully around and over the junk piled on the floor. Myron could hear her dialing the phone. Maybe she was right. It was time to bail out. If her father was home, he could come and get them. Myron had had adventure beyond his capacity to enjoy it. Uncle Hugo, Mr. Grinley, and Letitia Reticuli could work things out among themselves. Or not, for all he cared this evening.

Ms. Reticuli said, "I am delighted that your uncle Hugo was able to make the modifications on his nineteen sixty Chevrolet Belvedere. That particular model makes the best spaceship. Which is why I myself own one."

"Sure," said Myron without enthusiasm. "But why couldn't you modify your own nineteen sixty Chevrolet Belvedere?"

"Imagine," she said, "that your car broke down far from a gas station and you needed, say, a new distributor cap. Would you know how to build one?"

"I suppose not."

"Just so with me. I am a hot pilot. Not an engineer."

"Lucky that you found Uncle Hugo."

"The Ethical Structure of the Universe usually rewards those who have enough persistence. I have been searching for a man like your uncle Hugo for a long time."

"Good ol' Ethical Structure of the Universe."

"I wouldn't speak too lightly of it if I were you. Without the E.S. of the U., you would not have been able to escape from James Grinley and his henchpeople."

"I thought we were pretty clever," Myron said. Where was Princess? They had to get going even if they had to walk.

"Foxy for sure, child. Without your cleverness, even the E.S. of the U. would not have been able to save you. I would have had to step in sooner. And that would have drawn a lot more attention to us than we wanted."

"Attention?" Princess said as she returned from making her phone call, picking her way across the big crowded room. She nodded to Myron meaningfully. He did not know what she meant, but it seemed to token good news.

"Myron and I were just discussing your daring escape. If you had not been so resourceful, I would have had to rescue you. Chances are I would have had to blow up half the building to do it."

"With your ray gun, I suppose," Princess said. Her tone was not very polite. She was mighty confident about something, Myron thought.

"In a manner of speaking. I'd use the hand that you seemed so interested in." She held up her hand palm outward and it began to glow. It was much brighter than the yellow light that came from the electric bulbs on the sconces in the walls.

Princess moaned and her eyes got big. Myron was relieved that he had not imagined what had happened in Uncle Hugo's forest. He now also had good evidence for believing Letitia Reticuli's story. Which meant that they could believe Uncle Hugo's story, too. The pieces of junk Uncle Hugo collected probably *were* aliens after all. It meant that Mr. Grinley had to be stopped, not only to save Uncle Hugo, but to insure that the aliens got home safely.

Letitia Reticuli swung her hand around. It projected a palm-shaped patch of light onto a bedspring leaning in the corner. Suddenly Letitia Reticuli shouted, "*Eeyii!*" like some kind of ninja, and a flash zapped from her palm to the bedspring. The bedspring exploded in a flare of light so bright that Myron had to throw his arm over his eyes to protect them. The bedspring was gone. The only thing left was a charred outline against the wall where the frame and springs had been.

Myron and Princess jumped at the shout and the explosion. A few seconds later, Princess began to cry. This was a big surprise to Myron. Judging by her brave, well-timed actions that evening, Princess didn't seem like the type.

"Nothing to be afraid of, child," Captain Reticuli said kindly. "I would never do that to you."

"I know," Princess said through her tears, and wailed.

Captain Reticuli ran and got Princess a glass of water while Myron sat by watching her, unable to think of what to do. When Captain Reticuli came back, Princess took slow sips of the water. Soon the crying stopped, but she continued to sniffle.

"What's the story, Princess?" Myron said more gruffly than he had intended.

"I am a terrible person," Princess said as she dabbed her eyes with a tissue she had pulled from her pocket.

"Really," said Captain Reticuli as if she did not believe it.

"Really," said Princess. "I just called my Uncle James at Mr. Pinch's office and told them where we are." With that, she began to cry again.

"What?" yelled Myron.

"At work today, Uncle James asked me to be friends with Myron so that he could get more evidence to use against Myron's uncle Hugo. He told me it was for the good of the company. I thought it didn't matter because Uncle Hugo really was crazy, and Myron and I would just have a good time this evening. Besides, Uncle James threatened that if I didn't help him, he'd tell the Air Force that I'd been having lunch in the Tea Cup for the last six months. And now it turns out that Uncle Hugo isn't crazy and there really are aliens and I wouldn't mind going to prison for life if I could take back that phone call and I'm just miserable."

"But you helped me escape," Myron said.

Princess sniffled. "I was supposed to help you if you tried. Uncle James thought that would convince you I was on your side—"

"Humph," said Myron.

"—and you might lead me to some really big evidence against your uncle Hugo. If you didn't try to escape, or if you didn't succeed, he'd still have you in his clutches." Princess sniffled. "He'd win either way."

"I knew I should have gone with Poindexter alone," Myron said.

Princess was so miserable that she could only agree. Still sniffling, she said, "If my uncle James finds your uncle Hugo's nineteen sixty Chevrolet Belvedere, he'll get some kind of legal paper drawn up and have the car hauled off as evidence. Not only will Uncle Hugo be in big trouble, but the aliens will be stranded here forever."

Captain Reticuli said, "Princess, the important thing is that you told us now, before your uncle James and his friends show up. I would say we'd better get moving if we're going to escape them, warn Uncle Hugo, and get these puppies home."

"You mean blast off tonight?" Myron said.

"If the nineteen sixty Chevrolet Belvedere is ready, then Schyler and I are ready. We've been away from home for a long time. Besides, leaving the planet may be the only way to prevent Mr. Grinley from using the car as evidence."

"What about me?" Princess said in a shaky voice.

Captain Reticuli said, "You'll come with us, of course. I think you've learned your lesson." She and Princess looked at Myron. Princess was twisting her tissue into ribbons and fuzz.

Myron said, "Let's get moving."

The captain led them out her back door and down a flight of rickety wooden steps to an alley. Myron was carrying Schyler, the first officer who looked like a two-headed water main. Schyler was cold and heavy, and Myron almost dropped him a few times. At the foot of the stairway, Captain Reticuli's own white nineteen sixty Chevrolet Belvedere was parked against the back wall of the Unidentified Flying Omelet.

All three of them piled into the front seat, with the Captain behind the wheel. Myron held Schyler between his knees. Captain Reticuli started the engine. It roared, then settled down to a genteel ticking.

"Ready?" she asked.

"Ready!" said Myron and Princess together. Schyler said nothing.

"Spaceman's luck!" shouted Captain Reticuli as she gunned the engine and put the car into gear.

Before they could move more than a few feet, a car turned the corner at the far end of the alley and bounced toward them quickly.

"Someone looking for exotic omelets?" said Myron.

148

"We should be so lucky," said Princess.

The new car was a big black Lincoln. It blocked the alley and shone its headlights into their eyes. A man got out from each side of the car. One was Ivan. The other was Gert. They walked confidently toward the nineteen sixty Chevrolet Belvedere.

"Hang on," said Captain Reticuli. She threw the transmission into reverse, and they backed out of the alley like a rocket, jouncing into potholes and over lumps.

The nineteen sixty Chevrolet Belvedere zoomed out along Marsupial Boulevard. Seconds later, the black Lincoln was half a block behind and gaining.

CHAPTER FIFTEEN
JOBS FOR ALIENS

Captain Reticuli's driving was so wild, Myron braced himself against the dashboard, hoping he would survive the crash that was sure to come. He wished he'd been able to buckle up, but the Chevrolet Belvedere had no seat belts.

Schyler placidly rocked up and back between Myron's knees. No doubt, he and Captain Reticuli had been in tough situations before and he trusted her to get them out of this one.

Myron trusted her too, more than spit, at least, but his faith in Princess was utterly gone. He had agreed to allow her to come along because, first, arguing with her and Captain Reticuli would have taken time, and second, there were no telephones in the Chevrolet and Princess could not call Mr. Grinley again.

Myron glared at Princess. Her eyes were so red, she looked like a raccoon. She was still sniffling. It was possible that she really felt bad about spying for Mr. Grinley. But it was also possible that the tears were just more of an act. Myron was tired of puzzles. He glanced at his watch. It was getting on toward midnight. Suddenly, he was just *tired*—bone weary. When this was over, keeping his feet off Cousin Judy's furniture would be exciting enough for him.

Captain Reticuli was driving very fast and had managed to keep the lead, but the Lincoln was still half a block behind them. "Do something," Myron cried.

"I am about to," she said. She leaned forward and turned on the radio. Loud, fast, classical music came from it. "A little mood music," she said. "Just like in the movies."

"I hope that's not all," Myron said.

"Of course not." Captain Reticuli skidded the Chevrolet around the corner and down through the commercial section of Vasichvu Bend. The Lincoln was right behind them.

The streets and sidewalks were deserted. Light from the headlamps of the Chevrolet flashed on the plate-glass windows of small dark stores as the car zoomed past. Myron almost cried out when Captain Reticuli didn't try to escape down a really good dark alley between a shoe store—with the outline of a big red neon shoe in the window—and a tailor shop that had a half-lit plastic sign. He tried to feel the confidence that First Officer Schyler had in her. Then:

"Watch this," said the Captain as she squinted in

concentration. "Jobs for aliens," she said quietly, as if she were explaining something back in her apartment.

Suddenly, coins began to spew from parking meters on both sides of the street. They struck the Lincoln like machine-gun bullets, making a terrible noise. The Lincoln swerved from side to side as the coins blasted paint off its sides and cracked its side windows, but they didn't slow it down.

"They're still closing on us," Myron shouted.

"Aliens have many jobs," Captain Reticuli said. She hunched lower over the steering wheel. A moment later, Myron saw manhole covers spinning up out of their holes and rolling back toward the Lincoln.

"Wow!" Princess cried.

The manhole covers rolled right at the Lincoln, but the car turned suddenly, making a cover glance off its front bumper and crash into a parking meter, bending the meter pole in two.

"Casualty!" cried Myron.

"Brave soldiers," said Captain Reticuli.

The Lincoln wove between the other manhole covers, then between the open manholes. "Still coming," Myron said.

"Hmm," the Captain said. She turned up the music. The horns and violins seemed to become more frantic as their situation became more desperate. Myron mused, briefly, that some aliens might have gotten jobs as musical instruments.

Captain Reticuli cried out, "*Eeyii!*" like a ninja, as she had before.

Behind the Chevrolet, lampposts fell like big trees and rang like big gongs when they hit the concrete street. They were modern lampposts that each had two large cobra heads sticking out at an angle from the top. Myron could see how they were aliens.

They made a barrier that should have been impenetrable to an automobile the size of the Lincoln. The car had to slow down quite a bit, weaving along the length of one lamppost and then turning sharply and rolling down the length of the next one. This gave the Chevrolet a chance to get out of sight, but the Lincoln was still moving when they saw it last.

The city went from commercial to residential. Small dark houses lined the asphalt street. Every now and then a house had a light on on the porch, as if the house itself were waiting for someone to come home. Every time headlights shone in the back window of the Chevrolet, Myron and Princess turned and looked back. It was impossible to see what kinds of cars were following them, but each time, the car eventually turned into a driveway or into a cross street. Most of the time, the Chevrolet rolled through the dark streets alone.

"Do you think we lost them?" Princess said.

"No thanks to you," said Myron.

It was quiet in the car for a while. Captain Reticuli had turned down the classical music, and it was a rumble and a squeal in the background. Finally, Princess said, "What would you have done if your uncle Hugo had asked you, as a favor, to keep track of me?"

"I would . . ." Myron began, but he had to stop. What *would* he have done? He liked Uncle Hugo, despite the obvious fact that he was a wacko. Though Mr. Grinley was not a nice man, he *was* Princess's uncle. As much as he hated to admit it, Myron could see Princess's point.

"Tough decision," Myron said.

"Yeah," Princess agreed wholeheartedly.

They smiled briefly at each other.

Light shone in through the back window again. "It's them," Captain Reticuli said. "I guess they have a pretty good idea of where we're going."

"How do you know it's them?" Myron and Princess said together.

"Aliens are everywhere," the captain said. She turned the corner suddenly, throwing them all against each other. Seconds later, the car behind them screeched around the corner.

"That's pretty convincing," Myron said. He looked around. There were no parking meters, of course, and the lampposts in this part of town were the stubby cement kind. Even if they were aliens and could be made to fall over, they wouldn't block the street. "What are we going to do?"

"We need reinforcements," the captain said. She

drove through the side streets as if she were finding her way through a maze. They were going pretty fast, and it seemed as if they were going even faster because the streets were so narrow and dark. The Lincoln kept up easily. It would have caught them if it hadn't been forced to slow down so often when it rounded corners.

They passed an alley that touched the street at an angle. "There they are," said Captain Reticuli as she pulled over next to an old sprung couch that had threadbare arms. Slouching on the couch were three huge plastic trash bags, each one filled to bursting.

"Reinforcements?" Princess said.

"You bet. Those are Couch Potatoes from the planet Liebfraumilch. Come on. That car will find us in a minute." Schyler waited in the nineteen sixty Chevrolet Belvedere while the Captain, Myron, and Princess quickly got out. Each of them grabbed a Couch Potato. Captain Reticuli put hers down, pulled the seat forward, and hefted the bag into the backseat. She helped Princess with the second Couch Potato.

Before they could get the third alien loaded into the Chevrolet, the Lincoln roared around the corner and headed straight for them like a bomb.

Myron hurriedly passed the third Couch Potato to the captain. But before she could take it, the alien slipped from Myron's hands. The bag broke and rags, still sticky with fresh yellow and green paint, fell out and began to blow all over the place in the late night breeze. "Leave it," she yelled as she pushed Myron and Princess into the Chevrolet, then leaped in after them.

As they sped away, Myron looked out the back window. The Lincoln skidded to a stop where they had been only seconds before. Ivan and Gert leaped onto the street with raised pistols, but before they had a chance to fire, the colorful rags slapped against them, temporarily blinding them and covering their suits with paint. Other rags plastered themselves across the windshield of the Lincoln.

Captain Reticuli shook her head sadly. "That Couch Potato gave his life gladly to save the rest of us." She tapped Schyler with one finger and said, "Remind me to commend him in my log."

Schyler, as usual, said nothing.

"They'll never be able to find us now," said Princess, hopefully.

"They know where we're going," said the captain. "Our only hope is to get to Uncle Hugo's house and blast off before they can stop us."

They drove on. "Let me know when we get there, Myron," said Captain Reticuli. "You're the navigator here."

Myron nodded. He knew they were in Uncle Hugo's neighborhood because the houses were much farther apart than they had been, with big dark stretches of forest in between. Lamps hung from strong cables strung from one side of the street to the other. They hadn't seen lights behind them for a while, but the road tended to wander and anything could be hidden behind a curve or two. Besides, everybody in the Lincoln knew where the nineteen sixty Chevrolet Belvedere was going. It wasn't necessary to keep the car in sight.

"Not many aliens out here," Captain Reticuli said. "If we're going to get away from Grinley and his bunch, we'll have to do it ourselves."

"Turn there!" shouted Myron suddenly. He pointed off to one side. The captain nodded and turned the car up the gravel road onto Uncle Hugo's property.

The nineteen sixty Chevrolet Belvedere made a terrific crunching noise as it rolled over the gravel. The forest reared up on both sides of the car. If Myron hadn't known better, he would have thought he was lost in the wilderness.

The gravel road ran fairly straight, and it wasn't long before headlights were shining in the back window of the Chevrolet again. "How much farther is it?" Captain Reticuli asked.

"Not far," Myron said, hoping that he was remembering correctly. The Lincoln was getting closer. He could think of nothing between here and the barn that could slow it down.

CHAPTER SIXTEEN
WHO'S THE WACKO NOW?

The nineteen sixty Chevrolet Belvedere roared right past the mountain of junk that Uncle Hugo had piled up next to the gravel road. A few seconds later the road ended and the car skidded to a stop before the barn.

"That's the place," Myron said. "The modified nineteen sixty Chevrolet Belvedere is in there."

"Bring Schyler and the Couch Potatoes," Captain Reticuli ordered as she ran from the car to the barn.

Myron carried Schyler to the barn door while Princess dragged the two remaining Couch Potatoes over next to him. Myron could hear the hum of the Lincoln's engine now. It was getting closer. "Hurry," he cried.

Captain Reticuli was fussing with the big padlock but not getting anywhere. "Frooth," she swore. "Too bad this is a real lock and not an alien. Do you have a key?"

"Key?" cried Princess. "Just blast the sucker open with your hand!"

"I haven't got the energy to do a trick like that very often, child, and I'm saving what I have left for our friends in the Lincoln. Just in case Uncle Hugo's Chevrolet Belvedere is not modified *enough.* The key, Myron."

"Uncle Hugo has the only key that I know of. I'll go get him." He began to run toward the house but stopped when Princess called after him, "There isn't time." They could all see the headlights of the Lincoln now. She said, "Let's tear the boards off the windows."

Myron stood halfway between the barn and the forest not knowing what to do. He didn't mind tearing the boards off the windows, but that would take time too, maybe more time than getting Uncle Hugo.

Still, they had to do something. The Lincoln had about come to the turn in the road where the mountain of junk was. Captain Reticuli spun around, slapped her glowing hand against the air in the direction of the junk pile, and cried, "*Kreega!*"

Her hand flashed a solid white beam of light that slammed into the junk heap with an audible crash. Grating and groaning, a big avalanche of junk slid down on the Lincoln as it passed, stopping the car, burying it halfway up its windows. The car roared like an angry beast for a few seconds; then the motor ground to a stop.

159

"Run, child," said the captain. "Get your uncle Hugo. Tell him to bring his key."

Myron ran as fast as he could. There was no telling how quickly Mr. Grinley and all the rest might dig their way out of the Lincoln. Myron found the red-brick path, passed the tennis courts, and soon was running across the grassy slope behind the house.

Myron unlocked the kitchen door. Inside, he had no time to enjoy being in a familiar place again. He ran through the house and was about to run up the stairs to Uncle Hugo's bedroom, when Uncle Hugo himself came out of the libary. He was still dressed in his junk-hunting clothes, and he was holding an old rusty toaster in one hand.

"Myron!" he exclaimed.

"Uncle Hugo! You have to come to the barn right now. And bring your key."

"Why? What's going on? Where have you been? Why didn't you call?"

"I found the captain and the first officer. Mr. Grinley chased us. Please come now!"

Uncle Hugo felt in his pockets to make sure he had the key, and a moment later Myron was running back through the house with Uncle Hugo not far behind.

By the time they arrived at the barn, Pinch and Grinley and Ivan and Gert had recovered enough to shout at each other inside the car.

Letitia Reticuli and Princess had used their hands and

the Chevy's jack handle to pull boards off the windows, but the windows were nailed shut and they had made no further progress.

Uncle Hugo and Captain Reticuli shook hands and said how pleased they were to meet each other, but they did not spend a long time on pleasantries. Uncle Hugo unlocked the barn, went inside, and pulled the light chain. The light gleamed on the modified nineteen sixty Chevrolet Belvedere.

Myron kept looking over his shoulder while he pulled one of the Couch Potatoes into the barn. One door of the Lincoln had cracked open, and someone inside was pushing against it. The door didn't open very far, but it rocked the junk, making more pieces trickle onto the car. Myron heard more shouting.

Soon both Couch Potatoes were piled atop the junk in the backseat of the modified nineteen sixty Chevrolet Belvedere. Uncle Hugo and Captain Reticuli strapped Schyler into the front passenger's seat, his twin heads facing forward. Then the captain strapped herself in behind the wheel. She rolled down the window and shook hands with Uncle Hugo.

"Hugo, I don't know what to say."

"Then say nothing."

"What about the aliens who helped us?" asked Myron.

"And all the other aliens?" said Princess.

"I'll be back for them," said Captain Reticuli. "And

to get to know your uncle Hugo." She looked over her shoulder at the junk mountain outside. The others followed her gaze. The door of the Lincoln was open and four men were marching toward them. Mr. Grinley and Mr. Pinch were still wearing their gray suits. Ivan and Gert, their faces and suits smudged with yellow and green paint, had pistols.

"Spaceman's luck!" Uncle Hugo said as the captain rolled up her window. She started the engine. It sounded like a big insect. She waved as the car rolled forward.

"Stop that woman!" Mr. Grinley cried.

Myron wondered if he was talking to Princess. Princess did not seem inclined to cooperate. Along with Myron and Uncle Hugo, she did nothing but wave good-bye and cheer as the modified nineteen sixty Chevrolet Belvedere circled the barn and rolled smoothly through the grassy field behind it. Ivan trained his pistol on them while Gert fired at the Chevy. Bullets didn't seem to bother it.

Suddenly, sparks sputtered from the tailpipe, then a great feather of flame blasted from it. The entire car began to glow the way Captain Letitia Reticuli's hand had glowed earlier. And then it was no longer on the ground. It stayed level as it flew higher and higher. Then the insect hum rose to a shriek as the modified nineteen sixty Chevrolet Belvedere climbed steeply into the air and was soon lost among billions of stars.

Everybody watched it for a long time without saying anything. Ivan and Gert still had their pistols, but they seemed to have forgotten about them.

At last Uncle Hugo said, "Well, James, I guess that takes care of both our problems. I won't be buying junk anymore, so you won't have to take the company away from me."

"I want Astronetics," Mr. Grinley said. "This changes nothing." Mr. Pinch nodded in agreement.

To Myron this conversation was amazing. The three of them acted as if they were in some boardroom somewhere, not in the middle of a field having just seen a nineteen sixty Chevrolet Belvedere full of junk take off like a rocket.

Uncle Hugo said, "You'll have a hard time convincing people I'm crazy. Your main piece of evidence just took off for Liebfraumilch. If you tell anybody what you just saw, they'll think that *you* are crazy."

Mr. Pinch said, "We have witnesses to your earlier exploits."

"Who? Myron and Princess? They'll never cooperate with you two." Uncle Hugo laughed.

"They will," said Mr. Grinley. He smiled and said, "Perhaps they haven't told you about how we caught them doing lunch in the Tea Cup."

Uncle Hugo stopped smiling. Myron and Princess were looking at the ground. To them he said, "Is this true?"

Myron and Princess nodded without looking up.

Uncle Hugo said, "I don't know how to break this to you, James, but the barrel you seem to have them over is no barrel."

"Oh no? You know how secret the Tea Cup is. The Air Force will not be pleased. Myron and Princess will go to prison."

Myron was about to tell Mr. Grinley about the free-and-easy attitude that Clarence Terence O'melet had toward the Tea Cup, but he decided to save it for another time, when he could enjoy it more.

"I don't think so, James. As you may not know, General Gillooley, the head of the Tea Cup project, and I, are pretty good friends. I'll bet he would be delighted that Myron and Princess had found a security leak he can plug up."

Myron and Princess lifted their heads. "You think so?" they asked together.

"Sure. Grinley and Pinch have nothing on you."

"Don't forget to tell General Gillooley that neither of us is an Agent of a Foreign Power," said Princess.

"I won't forget."

"You're bluffing," Mr. Pinch said.

Uncle Hugo didn't even look at him. He only said, "You give the general a call. You'll find out if I'm bluffing."

Osgood ran out from among the bushes dressed in house slippers and a long blue robe that had a satin collar. "What's going on?" he began. He stopped suddenly when he saw Myron and Princess.

"Well," said Myron. "The Incredible Two-faced Osgood."

"What's this?" Uncle Hugo said.

Myron told his uncle about how he and Princess had followed Osgood to Cipher City with Art Poindexter. When Uncle Hugo found out that Osgood was in league with Grinley and Pinch, he was not pleased.

He asked Myron, "Why didn't you call and tell me about all this?"

"I did. But nobody answered."

"I was home all evening."

Myron, Princess, and Uncle Hugo glared at Osgood.

Pinch said, "As your attorney, Osgood, I advise you not to say anything."

"I'm sorry, sir," Osgood said. "I cut the wires."

Uncle Hugo said, "Does it surprise you, Osgood, that you are fired?"

"No, sir. I'll pack my things."

As Osgood walked off among the trees, Uncle Hugo said to Grinley, "And all of you can go with him. You can come back for your fancy car some other time." Uncle Hugo walked over to take a closer look at the car and the pile of junk under which it was buried.

Watching Ivan and Gert warily, Myron and Princess followed. But Ivan and Gert just stood around, holding their pistols as if they were vegetables. Mr. Grinley and Mr. Pinch were busy grumbling to each other in low tones.

Myron and Princess stood on either side of Uncle

Hugo who said, "I thought that mountain was made of *real* junk. But I guess they were aliens too, just waiting for the moment to help the cause."

"It could still be junk," Princess said. "Captain Reticuli knocked the mountain over with a blast from her laser hand."

Uncle Hugo nodded. "We may never know the truth."

"It's all part of the Ethical Structure of the Universe," Myron said.

"Absolutely," Uncle Hugo said. He walked across the gravel road, turned, and shouted to Grinley, Pinch, Ivan, and Gert. "If you're still on my land in an hour, I'll call the police." Chuckling, he entered the forest with Myron and Princess at his side. The moonlight made the trees look as if they were made of silver.

"You know, Uncle Hugo, there's still one thing I don't understand."

"There is?" said Princess.

"Yeah. The Tea Cup doesn't seem like the kind of thing a guy who believes in "sound engineering lines" would agree to build. How did you get it past Mr. Grinley and the others?"

Uncle Hugo chuckled again and said, "Good question. And I have a good answer. For one thing, I *had* to get it past them. The engine we developed for the Air Force's Tea Cup is the same engine that powers the modified nineteen sixty Chevrolet Belvedere. Without the Tea Cup, the aliens could never get home. For another thing, the government made the Astronetics board an offer they couldn't refuse. Big bucks were involved."

"I knew that money would figure in there someplace," Princess said.

Myron nodded. He felt good. He had helped Uncle Hugo. He had given Princess and himself an adventure that neither one of them would ever forget, and neither of them would have to go to military prison. Still, an entire summer was ahead of him, and keeping his feet off Cousin Judy's furniture no longer looked so appealing.

Myron said, "Now that the aliens have gone home, what will we do with the rest of the summer?"

"Yeah," said Princess. "I sure don't want to go back to Astronetics while Uncle James and Pinch work there."

"Not to worry," Uncle Hugo said. "I have another project in mind. You can both help me collect specimens." He put one hand on Myron's shoulder and another on Princess's. He said, "It involves very old objects and my new theory of *time travel.*"

What a wonderfully wacko idea, Myron thought. Not a "sound engineering line" in sight. This summer was going to be fun.